"Come," said the Duke, "let us have a sampling of what you give others so freely." He was suddenly aware that he had to take her in his arms. The sight of her burned him in more ways than he had ever imagined possible. His hands clasped her to him roughly as his mouth sought and took her own!

It was all Mandy had ever dreamed a kiss should be! Bubbles of intense emotion swept through her veins, melting her muscles until she felt herself go limp in his embrace. She had to remind herself that she loathed this savage libertine, that he was misusing her. However, her body and the effervescent state of her heart seemed to contradict such thoughts. She had to compellingly raise her hands and forcibly strike at his shoulders. And then, suddenly he was flinging her away from him, as though he no longer had use for her . . . no longer wanted that which he had taken!

"He is a madman," she thought to herself. "A madman." And all the while his kiss was engendering a depraved sensation in her heart.

Cotillion
for
Mandy

CLAUDETTE
WILLIAMS

FAWCETT CREST • NEW YORK

COTILLION FOR MANDY

Published by Fawcett Crest Books, a unit of CBS Publications, the Consumer Publishing Division of CBS Inc.

ISBN: 0-449-23664-1

Printed in the United States of America

10 9 8 7 6 5 4 3 2 1

Cotillion
for
Mandy

Chapter One

―――――――――――――――――――――――――――――――

"Lud!" declared a bright-eyed lady astride a good-looking prime blood stallion, "I do need this run. Come on Ned, let's wind it!" Her uncovered golden locks took to the air, waving in wild disorder at her back. Her brother released a sigh and sat back in his saddle. At a gentle application of his heel, his high-stepping roan bounded forward into a gallop, matching the lady's measure.

"Ho there, Mandy! I'm in no fit mood to take m'fences flying this morn. Want to talk to you," he said, reining in gently, slowing his horse to a trot.

She glanced sideways at his angular profile, so much like her own. She arched one dark brow slightly but slowed her horse and brought his gait to a complete stop. Her dark eyes looked into their mirrored image, for he was her twin, and more often than not they needed few words to understand one another's thoughts. There had always been a gentle harmony, deep-rooted, unassailable, and loving between them.

"What ails you, Neddy?" she asked gently. "You have not been yourself of late . . . though I can guess the cause," she added drily.

He shot her a sharp look and moved his gloved hand through his curly hair. " 'Tis Celia. Certes, Mandy, she has me fairly noddled!" he groaned.

"Ah . . . the wiles of a woman," chuckled Mandy, guiding her horse into a slow walk. "Pray, Ned . . . I don't want to be harsh with you, but it's time you took a good look at your fair charmer. Our lovely cousin plays fast and loose with you . . . bantling that you are, you see it not!"

Her brother did not appreciate this worldly-wise observation and exhibited his affront with deafening silence. His smaller twin sighed heavily. "Come Neddy, do not let us quarrel. You can't mean to get into a miff simply because I wish you to see the way of things."

"I ain't in a miff. What I am, is surprised! Surprised by your lack of faith in my judgment. As though . . . as though I'd let any skirt charm me into believing her better than she really is!"

"Then listen to me, my fine lad, and answer if you will," snapped his sister, her bright eyes flashing a challenge. "When you came home at Easter holiday and started fumbling for a place in our cousin's esteem, she was not at all interested. In fact, she did not even notice. I rather thought her attached to an-

other . . . seemed to have her head in the
clouds . . . but never mind that. As it happens, that
must be over, and lo, here you are again renewing
your attentions. But this time, the lady suddenly takes
an interest. Good Lord, Ned, she is two years your
senior . . . and *you* are about to attain your twenty-
first year and your full inheritance!"

A robust retort blustered through the light air.

"No such thing! That is a tarradiddle, m'girl. I'd
rather not speak on it any longer," he said, giving
her a stolid profile.

She sighed and attempted to win him over. "Neddy,
just think what it would be like to have Aunt Agatha
as mother-in-law." Her eyes were sparkling with
laughter and, had he been other than a brother, he
would have noted that her smile was as lovely as her
piquant face. However, although this appreciable fact
escaped Ned's notice, the field hand working nearby
took full note of it. The youth stood gaping with awe
at the beautiful young goddess on her dark horse. It
came to him suddenly that he might win a glance
from the lady if he could be of service, and dropping
his scythe, he rushed forward and unlatching the
staple, swung the single gate open for the riders to
pass.

This won him not only a glance, but a smile as
well. It blossomed in her dark eyes and warmed him.
The poor youth felt his breath abandon him as he stood
awestruck, until a rebuke from his older co-worker
called him back to his surroundings.

Ned waited until they had passed through the gate
before responding to her last remark, and this with
some fervor. "Aunt Agatha . . . *mother-in-law?*

Fiend seize such a notion and send it to perdition! Gadzooks, girl! Ain't going to marry Celia!"

"Well, then, my fine buck, what are you going to do with her? For I'm not green enough to think that all those lonely walks you two have been taking together are simply to admire one another from afar!" bantered Mandy, both brows uplifted.

He glanced sharply at her and then returned a sulky face to the road, "Devil fly away with me for a cad . . . for truth is, Mandy, I don't want to *marry* her!"

"Well, Ned, it's marriage the chit has in mind . . . depend upon it. And she is out to get it . . . one way or the other. And mind, now . . . I'd wager a pony she is not above using seduction, Neddy, m'lad," said Mandy on a knowing note.

He blushed to the roots of his pale gold hair and exclaimed in horrified accents, "Mandy!"

"Faith, Ned, think you are the only one up to snuff? Just because I haven't been to London for my Season, doesn't mean I don't know the way of things. She is out to get your name . . . mark me!" prophesied the lady.

He made no response to this, and they continued along the road on their way to Harrowgate village. Both were lost in thought, and neither paid any heed to the beauty of the landscape. The heather was near its glory and its purple held a tantalizing magic. Harebells danced in the summer breeze and invited admiration.

Mandy's thoughts were severely agitated—much more so than her bantering tone had indicated to her brother, the young baron, Edward Sherborne. Everything that troubled her led to Celia Brinley. Celia, tall, elegant, fashionable, secretive, and quite pretty, had come with her stepmother, Mrs. Agatha Brinley, directly after the funeral of Mandy's grandfather, a little over a year ago. Aunt Agatha had been regarded as a wayward daughter by the late baron, and had inherited nothing by his death. However, being a widow of limited means, she had made the decision to stay on at Sherborne Halls to look after the twins, who were at the time nineteen years of age.

It had been a sad time for both Amanda and Edward Sherborne. They had dearly loved their eccentric grandfather. Aunt Agatha's decision to stay on meant little to them at the beginning. Then it was time for Ned to return to Cambridge, but Mandy's plans to go to her maternal aunt for the London Season had to be canceled. She could not be brought out in her time of mourning. Thus, she remained at the Halls in the north of England. She loved the Dales country, and there had been much at the estate to occupy her time. But as the months progressed, Amanda Sherborne was growing restless. Now this problem with Ned and Celia had her nerves on end. It was true, she thought reflectively, Celia gave but little attention to Ned during his Easter stay. Even two weeks ago when Ned had first arrived she could not recall Celia's paying him much mind. This was a remarkable thing indeed, so Mandy thought at the time, for her twin was considered by many a fluttering heart to be a fair Adonis. In addition to his charming features, he was titled and soon to be wealthy. The secretive Celia had few prospects with her small dowry and her lonely situation up here in the Dales. She had been unable to afford a London Season, and even the most beautiful could be passed by if not seen by fashionable eyes. Then last week a slow change began to come over Celia . . . and it had increased substantially within the last two days. Celia was apparently awakening to Ned's many charms.

Now while Mandy concerned herself for Celia's motives, Ned did not. Celia's sudden interest pleased him to the point of abstract jubilation. He was about to embark upon the ripe and dangerous age of twenty-one. A man, thought he . . . in the next few months he would become a man! Very well then, Edward Sherborne, he asked himself proudly, what to do as a man? This reasonable if all-encompassing question left him puzzled. He had enjoyed being free, lover of women, a great gun to his many friends, and until yesterday he had not contemplated more than the usual larks a young man encounters during his summer holidays. However, his fair Celia soon brought him to task for his frivolous thoughts. Were they not in love? she demanded brutally. His answer was immediately reassuring. Well, then, did he not adore her? He contemplated this long enough to realize that the closeness of her certainly seemed to send his blood rushing through his veins in a most distracting way. Therefore he must suppose that he adored her. So he had answered. Very well, then, triumphed the fair maiden, it must next follow that two such creatures of their class, caught in the throes of such a miracle, must commit themselves to it before God . . . must they not?

Though a cloud had descended over Ned's dark eyes, his honesty usually prevailed, and he agreed with the above theory. Thus, it was he landed himself in the very muddle he now wished desperately to escape. Marriage! He had tried to explain to Celia the moment she had flung her arms about him with glee . . . saying to her disjointedly that it wasn't marriage he had had in mind. This brought on a fit of tears, and she accused him of not respecting her. How could he treat her so vilely when she had trusted him with her kisses . . . would trust him further should he so desire . . .

Ned Sherborne had a deep respect for womankind. He adored their lovely confusion of mind, and he thought he adored Celia. How then could he sit there and behave the cad, making her tears flow? He sought to comfort . . . what else could a young man like him do in a similar situation? Somehow, they had parted with Celia's kiss on his mind and her promise to seal their vows that evening by the lily pond. He wanted Celia . . . and knew that tonight he could have her . . . but . . . he did not want to *marry* her. The horrendous thought had kept him awake last night . . . and he did not look forward to their meeting this evening. But he would go, and he would tell her he did not want to marry her . . . indeed, he felt himself no longer really in love with her! He had wanted to tell Mandy . . . ask her advice . . . but then she had teased him and, though much of it rang true, he was not about to exhibit himself for a fool in his twin's eyes.

They were nearing the town, and Amanda glanced his way again. "Lud, but I thought the rain would never leave us. 'Tis good to have the sun smiling . . . even if it is a bit sultry."

"Eh? Oh . . . I suppose," said Ned absently.

"Aunt Agatha nearly drove me mad these last few days," Mandy went on, trying to draw him out.

"Lord, yes . . . Gadzooks, that woman does chatter . . . no wonder Grandpapa could never abide her company for long. One has only to say 'the pudding is good' for her to counter with, 'it's nought next to some' she has had," he chuckled, shaking his head.

Mandy laughed. "Indeed, yes. This morning when I chanced to remark that it was a good thing the sun had returned, for all that pelter of rain we've had was bad for the hay—she immediately offered me the comfort that it was worse for the wheat!"

"Bested again, Mandy! That'll teach you to trade with Aunt Agatha. Lud, but I'm weary of her. When do you think she'll take herself off?"

"Never, m'darlin' lad. She has freedom to act the great lady at the Halls, and she did grow up there after all. We mustn't be cruel," said Mandy, smiling gently.

"Good God, Mandy, I won't have it! I mean it is all very well for you to take the thing coolly . . . one day you'll marry some poor chap and take yourself off . . . and then . . . Gadzooks! I shall be stuck with Aunt for housekeeper . . . and I tell you, m'girl, I won't have it!"

Mandy laughed at his vehemence. "Goodness, Ned, you speak as though it might happen any day . . . my marrying and leaving the Halls, and I tell you it isn't likely!"

He grinned impishly. "Zounds, girl! You are nearly one-and-twenty . . . soon you'll be an old maid."

She pulled a face. "Odious brother! How should I

find my heart up here in the Dales? Oh, I grant you the moors were made for romance and knights to plod through to get to their loves . . . but *I* haven't found any that shine!"

"What of Sir Owen?" he teased, watching her closely.

She frowned at this. "Sir Owen is most certainly a gallant, and his charms are not lost on me, yet . . ."

"Yet what?" he persisted curiously.

"Have you never wondered what a rakehell . . . and, depend upon it, Sir Owen is a rakehell . . . is doing in the Dales of Yorkshire?"

"Don't need to wonder . . . know," said her brother, lording it over her.

"Well, then?" asked Mandy.

"Repairing lease . . . surprised you didn't guess. Didn't I just hear you declare you were up to snuff?" replied her twin glibly.

"Coming it a bit strong, aren't you? Repairing lease, indeed! He doesn't look burnt to the socket—from wine or any other questionable pleasure."

"Stoopid! He is hiding out from dun territory. Heard about it whilst I was at Cambridge. Lud! Nearly everyone is these days, what with taxes what they are and the banks so damn tight-fisted!"

"You mean he is in debt?" asked Mandy, surprised and suddenly deflated. It came to mind that the attractive Sir Owen may have been courting her for reasons having nothing to do with the heart.

"Not a sou to his name! Lost most of it on the gaming tables, they say. But he'll come about . . . his kind usually does."

"Brummell did not," said Mandy.

"No . . shame that! Things not the same, what with his name no longer leading the dandies. But seriously, though, Amanda . . . " he started, and she braced herself for his gravity. He always used her full name when he was about to be solemn. "'Tis time you had a London Season."

"I agree. Lud, Ned . . . I don't mean to complain, for I do so hate that sort of female. But the prospect of spending another winter with Aunt Agatha fluttering about my head . . . "

"Look here, m'girl. That quite settles it! What sort of brother do you take me for? Lord, that would be monstrous cruel. I'll set you up . . . see if I don't."

"Oh, Ned, if only you could. But truth is, you know you cannot. One needs a female sponsor for a season . . . for admittance to Almack's . . . and invitations to routs and such . . . and we have no connections in London." She sighed.

"Never mind that! I shall find some connections. Lord, girl, we'll have plenty of blunt . . . hire a chaperone . . . and I won't be so far off . . . come into town and escort you to the theater and all manner of things you will like."

"If only it could be contrived . . . but Ned . . . a hired chaperone, well . . . it's not at all the thing!" She sighed again. "And if I were to come to London, I should so want to be all the crack."

He pondered this problem a bit. "We do have a guardian, you know. Apply to him. After all, he is a duke. If anyone can see to it that you are well established, he can." He added, " 'Tis his duty!"

"Ha! He doesn't give a fig for duty. We haven't received word from him since his first letter after

Grandpapa's funeral. While that epistle may have been filled with good intentions, he never saw fit to carry them out!" replied Mandy somewhat bitterly.

"Odd that! I mean . . . he was Grandpapa's friend, wasn't he? Why would Grandpapa put our inheritance and our guardianship with someone who don't give a groat what we are about?"

"I daresay they had been friends in youth . . . I remember Grandpapa's solicitor saying something about the duke and Grandpapa having drawn up similar wills twenty years ago. What galls me is the duke's total *lack* of interest. I mean, really, he just gives over our estate into the hands of his agents and completely ignores our existence. And after such a nice letter!"

"It don't make sense, Mandy, blister it . . . it just don't!" He thought on this a moment. "I'll tell you what it is. The old codger is racked up with the gout. Can't do much when they're hit with it, I've heard," he added knowingly.

"Would serve him right if we racked up some scandal for him to stew in, Neddy, for gout or not, there is no reason why he couldn't have answered some of my letters."

"Never mind. We don't need him," said Ned dismissing the old fellow from his mind. "We'll come about."

She gave him a rather dubious look, but just then he stopped his horse at the edge of Harrowgate village before a gray tavern with a gay sign, indicating to all interested passersby that they had arrived at the Cock Pit.

Among the Cock Pit's many rustic charms, it boasted the best sport to be had for miles, this being the cock fight. In addition to the tavern room on the main floor, it housed a large gallery room whose center exhibited a round, slightly raised theater. About this wooden platform were benches now filled with quality gents, cits, and skirters. The betting was rife, the ale was flowing, and spirits were high with expectation.

Ned dismounted, his smile broad in greeting to a group of young blades hailing him from the tavern window. "Well, Mandy, old girl, I'm off. If you want m'company home, you'll have to keep yourself occupied for at least two hours. For, depend upon it, this cocking will take the good part of an hour, and it's not due to start for a bit yet."

She grimaced. "Must you attend such a horrid thing, Neddy?"

"Now don't be missish. . .ain't like you," chided her twin. "Must I attend indeed?" he grunted, apparently feeling this was a stupid question. "Skippy has his red entered in this fight, and I've wanted to see Wally's gray bleed these two years and more!"

"Bloodthirsty thing!" cried his sister with a laugh. "Well, then, give Skip my love and wish his horrid red luck, for in truth I don't like Mr. Wallington and should like to see him lose." With this Mandy urged her stallion on toward Harrowgate's small but busy center.

Chapter Two

Dusk wrapped its smoky billows over the Dales and, though it was a warm summer evening, Celia Brinley hugged her blue shawl tightly about her well-shaped shoulders. She fidgeted on the cold stone bench as she peered thoughtfully into the blackness of the lily pool at her feet. Her reflection came back to her, and she smiled in approval, not only for her appearance but for her plan as well. She was meeting Edward Sherborne tonight.

She would allow him to think *he* had seduced *her*, and she knew just how to accomplish such a feat. He was a babe to be manipulated. It was necessary, for she had to think of herself. She had to plan for her future, and once he had taken her, he would give her his name. And she needed Lord Sherborne's name. Her hand went almost instinctively to her still flat stomach, and she cursed—first herself and then another. That wretch—that wicked, deceitful wretch. How she had loved him, openly, wantonly, faithfully, but now she knew, she had just been a diversion. He would not marry her and give their child a name. He had told her so last week, and she had been stunned by his reply. But, now . . . she had a way to revenge herself upon him. She would gain for herself a wealthy husband, a father for her child—and she now had a means to destroy the blackguard. She had met him yesterday just to watch his expression when she told him what she knew. Her reverie was interrupted by the sound of a soft footstep. She looked up, her blue eyes widening with surprise.

"What are *you* doing here?" she exclaimed.

Ned had excused himself from the dinner table earlier than was his habit, leaving Mandy to suffer their chatty aunt alone, for Celia had taken dinner in her room. Soon, Mandy's manners ebbed, and she rose, making a lame excuse and leaving her aunt to linger over her second helping of peaches and cream.

She wandered to the front parlor, a room that jutted out onto the front lawns at a right angle. It had a window seat where a collection of plants reposed in green array. Mandy slipped in amongst these and gazed out the diamond panes, wondering where Ned and Celia had gone . . . for she was nearly positive they had gone off together. She remained thus until Roberts announced the arrival of Mr. Alfred Speenham. This piece of news drew a resigned sigh from

Mandy and brought her head round. It was easy enough for her to smile in spite of the fact that this particular visitor was not welcome, for Mr. Speenham's figure often inspired a grin. Her dark eyes found a thickset young man of average height whose light brown curls gleamed with pomade and whose features seemed blurred in his puffed countenance. He wore white-topped boots, a florid waistcoat with dozens of fobs, and a long-tailed coat of bright blue that sported enormous brass buttons.

Alfred Speenham was a cousin. His father had married into the maternal side of the family, received his one spawn before becoming a complacent widower. They lived some miles to the south of Sherborne Halls and were more often than not popping in and out.

With regard to these relations, Mandy was unsure of only one thing—which of the two she held in greater contempt—father or son.

"Amanda darling . . . how divinely angelic you do appear framed in all that verdure," said Mr. Speenham, smiling and coming across to her. "It suits you . . . most certainly it suits you."

"Do you think so? I wonder how I may contrive to have just such a background when I move about— since it finds favor in your eyes," returned Mandy drily.

He smiled indulgently. "Now you are jesting with me again, Amanda. Are you never serious, Cousin?"

"I am always serious, Alfred," retorted Mandy, her expression unfathomable.

He narrowed his hazel eyes sharply, for he was never quite certain what she was thinking and always had the peculiar sensation that she was laughing at him.

But how could she? Really—he thought complacently, it was obvious he was a fine figure of a man. She should be flattered that he noticed her at all. Actually, Mr. Speenham was not overly fond of his cousin Amanda. His father incited his visits to Sherborne, threatening to cut him out of his will if he did not comply. For his part, Alfred Speenham was quite satisfied to remain a bachelor, though for a time he had wanted Celia Brinley.

He moved casually, taking up a seat. "I spotted Ned on my way up the drive."

"Oh?" said Mandy, interested. "Alone?"

"Yes . . . why?" he returned, frowning and curious.

"Did you speak with him?" pursued Mandy, ignoring his question.

"Funny thing that. Thought he saw me, too . . . but couldn't have for he darted right to the thicket . . . toward the lily pond near the main road. Wouldn't have done that if he had seen me . . . would he now?"

"Of course not, Alfred," she replied gravely. "But tell me . . . what brings you to Sherborne?"

"You," he said brazenly. Amanda Sherborne found his monosyllabic reply exquisitely humorous and burst into laughter. Her cousin glared at her, wondering what she could find amusing in his gallantry.

"You find that funny?" he asked.

She dabbed at her eyes with her lace handkerchief and gazed across at him, her eyes brimful with mirth, "Should I not, Cousin?"

"I don't see why you should," he retorted, his tone much peeved.

"Now, Alfred . . . you know very well 'tis Celia you look for . . . not me."

"Well . . . that is how much you understand of the situation. Celia never held m'heart! She was just . . . for sport," he said callously.

"You horrid thing! Why, it would serve you right if I were to repeat that to Aunt Agatha . . . or to Celia herself."

He looked round nervously. "Where are they anyway?"

"I don't know," said Mandy coldly.

"Now, Amanda, needn't get into a huff . . . and no sense threatening to go to Aunt Agatha with what I chance to say . . . 'twould only cause her to get into a pucker. But really . . . where is Celia?"

"I . . . I don't know . . ." said Mandy carefully. "Why?"

"Had this note from her . . . rather, m'dad had this note from her . . . requesting him to attend her tonight at eight. He couldn't come so he sent me instead."

"So that is why you are here."

"No, no, 'tis only a few minutes past seven!" he retorted quickly. "Came early . . . to spend time with you."

An idea struck Mandy, and she moved across the room, allowing her fingers to stray idly over the sofa back. "So then you must remain till after dark . . . how horrid for you. This means you must needs ride home at such a late hour."

"Now just a moment, Amanda." said Alfred sitting up straight. "Do you mean to imply that I, Alfred Speenham, might be afraid of the dark?"

"Certainly not! Are you not your father's son?" she retorted, knowing her mark, for it was a well-established fact that Squire Bevis Speenham had several fears, one being the absence of light.

He glared at her suspiciously. "Well, *I* have no qualms about riding home from Sherborne after dusk."

"No? Has the main pike been repaired then?" asked she, knowing full well it had not been.

"No, but what has that to do with anything? 'Tis but a mile longer on Abbey road."

"Yes, but you needs must pass Bolton Abbey ruins," said Mandy ominously.

Mr. Speenham had not thought of that, but he poohed it away, "Bosh! It doesn't signify!"

Mandy was not daunted. She had a naughty sense of fun and a ready imagination to further it. "I for one have not gone near the ruins after dusk . . . not since Lady Hatfield's recent experience."

"Eh? Lady Hatfield's experience?" he asked warily.

"I don't know that I should be telling you this. After all I don't want to make you nervous on your ride home," said Mandy.

He snapped his fingers in the air. "Nonsense . . . nervous indeed! Now what happened to Lady Hatfield?"

Mandy sat down opposite her cousin and freely began her fabrication, adding half-truths to the lie to give it the aura of reality. "It was already dark when they passed the abbey ruins . . . and then suddenly . . . " shouted Mandy, flinging her arms up for emphasis and causing her cousin to start. Then lowering her voice ominously, she continued in a hushed whisper, "Suddenly . . . from over the abbey's west wing they heard an unearthly cry . . . a wail of some sort . . . and looked up to find a wolf poised on the crumbling ledge."

"A wolf . . .?" cried Mr. Speenham in doubt. "There are no wolves in the area."

"Precisely!" agreed Mandy, "and this one glowed! And faith! His howl . . . it was the sound of death!"

"The . . . the sound . . . of death?" Mr. Speenham's eyes were wide while his voice took on a nervous pitch. "I . . . I am not acquainted with . . ."

"Nor were Lady Hatfield and Chauncy. Yet make no mistake—it was the sound of death! It sent shivers up their spines, and you know that my man Chauncy is not one to run . . . yet when the chains started rattling . . ."

"Chains?" said Alfred with some agitation.

"Indeed . . . chains . . . followed by a cry of horrendous pain. Well, he thought it best to get Lady Hatfield home without further delay."

Mr. Speenham gulped as he digested Mandy's elaborate story. "Pray, Amanda . . . I have no wish to disturb your peace of mind regarding my safe journey home. I have decided to stay the night at Sherborne!"

Amanda's dark eyes opened wide, perceiving the error of her madness. "Stay here? Oh, no, Alfred . . . you could not wish to do such a thing. Why your father will be expecting you home."

"Bosh!" said Alfred. "He will assume that I have remained the night at the Halls . . . and at any rate you can send a lackey with a message to him."

"Well, Alfred, really!" said Mandy putting her hands to her hips, "If we can send a lackey past the ruins without fear for his life, then there is no reason why you can't go home without fear for yours."

"Don't see that. Don't see that at all," said Alfred,

thinking she had little sensibility. "Ghosts and such creatures wouldn't bother with a mere lackey . . . but a Speenham . . . well . . . stands to reason that the fiendish things would want a crack at me."

She eyed him fulminatingly a moment. "Indeed, yes."

He rubbed his hands together quite pleased at the outcome. "Amanda darling, do you think you could ring for some refreshments?"

Sir Owen Turndale rounded the corner of the main road, easing his large bay up the winding drive of the Sherborne estate. He had in his pocket a note from Miss Celia, but unlike the note to Squire Bevis Speenham, it requested Sir Owen's presence at the Halls at precisely seven-thirty that evening. He hurried his horse, for it was already considerably past that time. He allowed his mind to dwell on Celia's image. Gad, but she was a dainty piece and had showed herself quite a willing one as well! But enough of that, it was *Miss Amanda*'s heart he sought.

He pulled at his beaver top hat, setting it rakishly over his auburn curls. Sir Owen had come up from London about four months ago on what he loosely termed a repairing lease. The sorry truth was that the handsome rakehell had landed himself at *point non plus*. Though his address, his nature, and inclination were for the London set and not his ancestral moorland estate, his pockets were to let. He had gambled away his meager fortune, had mortgaged his land in order to pay his debts of honor . . . and now he was hiding out from the tradesmen.

Ordinarily, Amanda Sherborne's lively good looks

and unsophisticated manners would have caught Sir Owen's eye for a passing moment. However, he soon learned that she was an heiress and soon to come into her own. It was then that he set out to charm his way into Amanda's heart. He congratulated himself that his efforts had not been totally in vain. He would have been sadly taken aback had he known the way of it, for Amanda, while flattered, amused, intrigued, perhaps a bit enchanted, was not in love.

He pursued her sedulously and soon found that her volatile expressions, her innocent eruptions of pleasure, and her adorable countenance were even more pleasing than he had at first realized. As of late his attentions had been redoubled, and it was with eagerness that he awaited the right moment to finalize his endeavors. He often contemplated marriage with Mandy and, though he was certainly taken with her pulchritude, her dark eyes and golden hair, he knew himself enough to realize that marriage would not sit well for long! Had Amanda perhaps allowed her bubbling joy to emit fire, had she permitted at least one of his many advances to arouse passion, or engender at least a warm response, his hardened heart might have moved, but no such fire had been lit in her, and his heart remained intact.

His eyes of marsh brown caught the movement of someone up ahead on the drive, and he recognized Alfred Speenham. This brought little surprise to Sir Owen's mind, though his mobile brows went up thoughtfully. Just then he caught sight of Ned Sherborne dashing into the thicket, and he smiled to himself. However, he had no time for speculation. The sound of a heavy object crashing brought his head round a few moments later. He stopped and speaking softly to his horse, dismounted. He tethered the animal to a birch tree, before following the young Lord Sherborne down the path to the lily pond. Some minutes later he brought himself up short at the sight of Ned hovering over Celia's still form.

"Hold there, lad, what have we here?" said Sir Owen, frowning as he came forward to investigate.

Ned turned strained, horrified eyes upon the newcomer and finding there Sir Owen, someone to rely on, he groaned, "It's Celia! My God! She has been stabbed!"

Sir Owen was leaning over her in a moment, and his voice when it came was strange. "Indeed . . . she has been stabbed. And I am afraid . . . is quite dead."

"Oh . . . my God! Dead?" breathed Ned running a hand through his hair. "But who . . . why?"

Sir Owen scanned the surroundings quickly, allowing his eyes to linger on a statue of Venus lying broken upon the ground, its head shattered, its body in the pond.

"May I ask, Lord Sherborne, whether this statue was in its present situation when you first arrived on the scene?'"

"Statue?" asked Ned, his eyes still on Celia's inert form. "Statue? Oh! No, no. I saw Celia and ran to her . . . I knocked it over in my haste."

"I see. It was that, then . . ." said Sir Owen to himself.

"What?" said Ned.

"Nothing . . . it just explains what I heard," he sighed heavily. "Then, Miss Brinley was as we see her when you first arrived?"

"Yes."

"May I ask how you happen to be here?" asked Sir Owen eying Ned oddly.

"If you must know, I had an assignation with Celia for seven-thirty this evening. We had something . . . to discuss."

Sir Owen's brow went up. "Really, my lord? How odd . . . seven-thirty. Now why would the young woman make an appointment with two gentlemen for the same time . . . at different locations?"

"Dear God! What are we doing . . . standing here talking in this insane fashion? Blister it, Owen! Someone has stabbed Celia!" thundered Ned in disbelief.

"Indeed . . . someone has . . ." said Sir Owen, casting another glance over her limp body, finding that even in death her face was quite, quite lovely.

Some hours later, the servants and household were in a state of buzzing commotion. The doctor had arrived and added yet more distressing information to the awful announcement that Miss Celia Brinley had indeed died from the wound made by what (lacking firm evidence) he supposed to be an ordinary knife plunged near to her heart. He advised the assembled company that Miss Brinley had been approximately three months pregnant. This piece of news served to prostrate Celia's step-mother, and Mrs. Brinley was taken in hysterics to her room where she was given a sedative.

Having stayed with her Aunt Agatha until the prostrated woman went to sleep, Mandy now entered the library. Her lovely face was drawn and her complexion pale. The trouble in her bosom showed in her dark eyes, and Sir Owen noted it with some concern.

He watched her from the corner of his eye and thought it wise to be solicitous. He came forward, glass in hand, and offered it to her. "Take this, Amanda . . . it will help."

She declined the potation wearily and dropped down upon the sofa next to her brother. His head was sunk morosely in his hands, and she put her arm about his slumped shoulders. He lifted his face and glanced sideways at her. Their eyes met in gentle understanding.

"Amanda," began Alfred irritably, "now that Aunt Agatha is settled in her room and out of hearing . . . *we must talk!*"

"Oh, Alfred, do stop always trying to sound so portentous! Why must we talk?" Amanda's voice was testy. All she wanted was to be left alone with her brother. If there was talking to be done, she thought it to be between them.

"The seriousness of this situation absolutely demands it, Amanda, so, indeed, your flippancy is out of place," scolded her cousin. "Don't you realize . . . it will be all over the county by morning?"

"Indeed, unfortunately, Mr. Speenham is correct in that," agreed Sir Owen.

"Obviously there will be talk. But what can we do about it by hashing it amongst ourselves?" asked Mandy.

"Amanda," said Sir Owen gently, "it has become evident that Miss Celia had . . . a lover . . ."

"Yes, and that he killed her!" put in Alfred with some agitation.

"Why would a lover kill her?" asked Mandy dubiously.

"Jealousy!" returned her cousin. "Why else? They do, don't they? Well . . . not very much any more . . . at least, not in England, but it was the thing at one time . . ."

"Oh, do shut up!" interjected Ned stingingly. "Of all the foolish . . ."

"Just a moment, Sherborne," put in Sir Owen. "It is likely, that for quite a different reason—one the doctor pointed out to us tonight—this lover found it necessary to dispose of Celia."

"Oh, my word, Sir Owen, what are you saying? That some man, some mystery man . . . killed Celia rather than marry her?"

"What other explanation is there?" said Sir Owen, shrugging his shoulders. "However, there is still something very strange about this entire affair. I should like to try to clear something up before we say good-night . . . with your indulgence, Miss Amanda."

"Oh, very well . . ."

Sir Owen turned to Alfred Speenham. "You say you . . . or rather, your father received a note requesting him to attend Miss Brinley tonight at eight?"

"Yes, but what the deuce . . .?"

"Isn't that odd? Your father and Miss Celia were not . . . overly fond of one another. Why would she request his presence?"

"I don't know . . . what the . . .?"

He cut him off again, "Then, too, she requested my presence here at seven-thirty. Yet her appointment with Ned was for 7:30. Why?"

"Indeed . . ." Sir Owen pulled at his lower lip. Returning to Mr. Speenham, he said, "Are you certain the note called for eight o'clock?"

"Of course, I am certain. Here, I'll show you." he answered, reaching into his inner pocket. When his hand came out empty, he patted his chest and frowned. "Now where did I put it? I am quite sure I had it, for when Skippendon wanted my wager signed . . . I know I had it . . . held it in m'hand . . ." he said, trying to recall the incident.

"Skippendon?" inquired Sir Owen.

"Yes . . . you know, the viscount . . . met him today at the Cock Pit."

"Ah, yes. Had a look in there myself."

"What the devil does all this about notes and such matter?" asked Ned irritably.

"It matters, my lord," said Sir Owen gently. "Now we cannot locate Mr. Speenham's missive from Celia. Shall we move on?" He took their silence for acquiescence and continued, "May I ask Lord Sherborne how you arranged your meeting with Celia for tonight?"

"Devil fly away with you, Owen . . . don't like this," said Ned.

"Why?" asked Sir Owen, his brow going up.

"Don't see its purpose," replied Ned impatiently.

"You will, my lord," said Sir Owen gravely. "Now you needn't answer, but I think it will help if you do."

"Very well. Celia had asked that I meet her by the pond at seven. That was the original plan. Then I received a note from her just after dinner, telling me to be at the pond at seven-thirty instead."

"May I see that note?" said Sir Owen quietly.

Ned dived into his chest and produced a crumpled piece of paper. Sir Owen produced the note he received from Celia and compared them. His brows went up and he gazed at Ned in surprise. "These were not written by the same hand."

"What?" ejaculated Ned and Mandy at the same time. "But what does it mean?"

"First, we shall have to determine which is Miss Celia's writing," said Sir Owen, handing the notes to Mandy. "I daresay *you* would recognize her writing."

Mandy frowned over the notepapers and then sighed. "I . . . I cannot be certain, but your letter appears to be written by her hand, Sir Owen."

Again, he turned to Ned. "Who brought you this note, my lord?"

"Her maid."

Mandy went to the bellpull and gave it a hard tug. A moment later a lackey appeared, and she ordered him to call Celia's maid to them at once. But as she joined Ned on the sofa again, she realized what the fear in her heart had been.

"I am afraid I shall have to ask you, my lord," said Sir Owen quietly, sadly, "were you the father of Miss Celia's child?"

Ned jumped to his feet, "Fiend seize you, Sir Owen! How dare you! What sort of scoundrel are you making me out to be? Damn, but I have a notion to call you out."

"Stop, Ned, do stop," cried Mandy, tugging at his arm. However, she rounded on Sir Owen angrily. "I must say, sir, that I am both hurt and shocked at your question."

He looked long and imploringly at her. "Please, Miss Amanda, do not look so at me. It had to be asked. I never thought so for a moment, but it had to be asked and put away."

Suddenly, Mr. Speenham's eyes narrowed, and a feeling of satisfaction swept him. Of course, everyone was bound to think Ned the father of her child. His courtship had been so indiscreet that half the county was talking about it and laying odds he'd be caught before the end of the summer. Why hadn't he realized that earlier?

"Good lord!" he ejaculated now. "This should be reported to m'father. Magistrate, you know."

"Oh, for goodness' sake!" breathed Mandy. "The doctor said he will take care of that in the morning."

"Can't wait till morning. And besides . . . he will need more details than the doctor can give," said Speenham ominously.

A knock sounded on the library doors and a lackey appeared, his eyes wide with his news. "Miss," he cried, "Elly Bonner . . . Miss Brinley's maid . . . she be not 'ere. Up and left . . . and done took all her things, she did."

"Thank you," said Mandy with a sinking heart. She waited for the man to leave before turning to her brother. "Oh, Ned, why would Elly take off like that?"

"I don't know. I just don't know," he answered fretfully.

Mr. Speenham moved across the room. "I'm off. You will come, won't you, Sir Owen? After all . . . you found m'cousin here with Celia."

"Do shut up, Alfred," said Mandy impatiently.

"Look here, that's no way to speak to me. It's Ned here that has gone and got himself mixed up in the blackest scrape ever I've seen, not I," he said testily.

Ned jumped to his feet and took a menacing step towards him. "Fiend seize your shriveled soul, you puling noddy!"

Mr. Speenham hastened away, then turned back at the door to wait for Sir Owen as he suddenly remembered that he would have to pass the Abbey ruins and dreaded doing so alone. "Do you come, Sir Owen?"

"If only to keep you from distorting the facts to your father," replied Sir Owen. He turned and bowed low over Mandy's hand. "Believe me, your obedient servant in this . . . and all things, my love."

She pulled her hand away coldly. She had not liked his questions. She had liked them even less in front of Speenham who would not have been rushing off to fill his father's ears with the answers had not Sir Owen dissected the situation for his edification.

"Good-night, Sir Owen," she said, dismissing him.

Brother and sister waited until they were sure the two men had left the house before turning to one another. Mandy was upset and, though she tried to hide it, her tone was still agitated when she spoke. "Ned, I don't like the insinuations behind Owen's questions."

"Nor do I. What's more, m'girl, there were a dozen or more questions he didn't ask. But I felt them all the same, and it sent a spooky sensation through me. This whole thing is too smoky by half . . . and damn if I have any answers."

"We need help . . . and there is but one person I know of that can offer it. In the morning we'll ride over to Skippendon," suggested Mandy.

"Skippy?" Ned brightened. "Certes, Mandy, you've hit upon the very thing! Skippy will see us through this."

Abovestairs, Mrs. Agatha Brinley's troubled eyes moved about her room. It had been a dreadful ordeal. These last few months had been a horror for her. Now

Celia was gone! Thank goodness, she thought piti-
lessly. Celia was gone, and with her stepdaughter's
death her fears died also.

Sir Owen rode silently abreast Mr. Speenham. He
was thoughtful for several reasons. One was the fact
that the lady he sought to wife was annoyed with him.
So be it. He would soon bring her round. He had a
way with women, and Amanda was very much a
woman. The other thoughts had much to do with the
future, for by morning the Sherborne family would be
flung into scandal. He had no liking for that, but it
would appear there was nothing for it. And Celia . . .
she but entered his mind fleetingly, for he had
enjoyed . . . but never mind that, he told himself,
his heart coldly flinging all memory of her aside!

Mr. Speenham's eyes became watchful as they
neared Bolton Abbey ruins. Its irregular walls loomed
over the heather field, and he could see its silhouette
casting ominous shadows into the glen. He encouraged
Sir Owen to hurry past its dark stones, for it seemed to
be laying in wait for prey. Once safely past this stretch
of glen, Alfred's thoughts flitted over Celia's image. It
was too bad, really, he thought, for he had thought her
so classically beautiful. He sighed, and then remembered that it was Ned who was finally in trouble. That
was a stroke of good fortune. At last, he would be able
to lord it over his haughty cousin, Edward Sherborne.
This fancy gave him a great deal of pleasure and he
let his thoughts dwell on this future prospect.

Chapter Three

Viscount John Skippendon's home lay some miles southwest of the Sherborne estate. The extensive Wharfedale Manor grounds skirted a narrow channel through which the waters of the Wharfe poured its silver rills. Mandy had always admired Wharfedale's natural beauty and the fine artistry of the viscount's gardeners, who used their skills wisely to enhance nature. However, this morning found her eyes unseeing and her mind occupied with thoughts that had nothing to do with beauty. How would she convey to Skippy the sort of scrape they were in? What would he think? What would he do?

Skippendon's holdings, his fame, and his heart were known to be vast and wide open. He was a favorite both in and out of London, though recently the *haut ton* of London had been neglected for the wilds of Yorkshire. He was a beloved friend to the twins in spite of the five years' seniority he had over them. They looked upon him as an older brother, delightfully amusing, wise, and most certainly knowledgeable—if not in all things, certainly in a great many. This blind faith in Skippy would have most assuredly startled his many fashionable intimates, for while these worthies unanimously smiled upon the lovable viscount, none of them had ever looked to him for wisdom!

"Good thing Skip is still at Wharfedale," said Ned with an accompanying nod of his head.

Mandy pushed the white scarf of her blue silk top hat away from her neck and sighed. There was little breeze, and the day was already promising to be sultry. "Indeed yes. Lud, but he has been at his manor now some . . . six months. I've never known him to stay away from London for such a protracted time. But never mind. 'Tis fortunate for us that he has, for I tell you quite frankly, Neddy, I don't like what is happening up at the Halls. Aunt Agatha behaved most oddly this morning, and I had no liking for the manner in which Alfred stalked out last evening."

They slowed their horses to a walk as they approached the viscount's stables. Two young stable boys came rushing toward them, and a moment later they had dismounted, and their steeds were being led away. Mandy smoothed out the wrinkles in her blue silk riding habit and put up a kid-gloved hand to pat her bright gold curls. Ned fidgeted as he waited for her to complete her toilette. "Come on, girl. Lud, you look all right."

She pulled a face but fell in step beside him. A stony-faced butler stood before them a moment later, and Ned cheerily dropped his hat and gloves into the man's hands. They were led across the shiny oak floor of the dark Tudor hall to a pair of heavily moulded doors. These opened into a brightly furnished morning room, and as the viscount looked up from the coffee he was sipping, he both heard and saw Mandy Sherborne. She squeaked his name and came forward with a wild rush, scarcely giving him time to stand. He wore a brocade dressing gown over his shirt sleeves and breeches, and Mandy dived into his arms, crying his name again, "Skippy . . . oh, Skippy!"

Ned found nothing unusual in his sister's unconventional behavior and he proceeded to pounce upon the chocolate tart he discovered on the viscount's tray. This in hand, he plopped himself unceremoniously into a near-by chair, whereupon he made short work of the sweetcake.

The viscount took strong exception to the attack. Putting Mandy away from his lean chest with a sharp "What's this, girl?" he glared at Lord Sherborne. "Hold there, you scoundrel! That's the last tart!"

"Is it? Well then, you have the satisfaction of knowing it has been appreciated," grinned Ned, not in the least abashed.

Viscount Skippendon shot him a fiendish look but, as Mandy was tugging at his sleeve, returned his attention to her with a groan. "May I know to what I owe this unexpected . . . and most unwanted pleasure?"

"Don't be horrid, Skippy . . . for we are in the most dreadful straits!" said Mandy, her dark eyes unamused.

"Eh . . . what's this?" asked the viscount, his pale blue eyes opening wide.

"Aunt Agatha's stepdaughter—Celia—was murdered last night," Mandy continued in a hushed whisper.

The viscount dropped into the yellow brocade Chippendale chair he had occupied prior to the twins' arrival. "Good God!"

"Precisely," said Ned, sitting forward and clasping his hands between his knees. "Skip, *someone stabbed her!*"

"Never say so! Upon my word!"

"Exactly," said Mandy, "But—that is not the worst of it."

"No? What more can happen after murder?" Skippy paused. "What the deuce do you mean that ain't the worst of it?"

"She was . . . with child . . . three months, the doctor says," replied Mandy, blushing.

"Blister it, Mandy! Was he sure?" asked Skippy, frowning. "I mean . . . really . . . did he have to say so? Terrible thing that. Tongues will wag as it is. Did he have to add to it?"

"Skip, she was murdered. I mean it matters . . . doesn't it?" Mandy eyed him meaningfully.

Realization dawned on him, and his blue eyes opened as the thoughts took form in his mind. "Gadzooks! Yes, it does!" He pulled at his thin lower lip a moment and then sighed, "Well . . . nothing for it. We shall have to weather it out. Bound to be a great deal of prattling about the thing. Perhaps it would be a good notion for you two—and your aunt—to take a jaunt to London. Just until the tattlemongers have had their fling."

"Blister it, you are not getting the gist of it at all," said Ned impatiently. "First of all, Celia was murdered. We must do something to find her murderer."

"Don't see that . . . don't see that at all!" snapped the viscount with a shake of his sandy head. "Leave that to the runners."

". . . and if I may continue," said Ned with irritation giving his words bite, ". . . it appears that *I* am suspect."

"*What?*" shouted the viscount, jumping to his feet. "Preposterous!"

"It is, of course, absurd. But you see, Neddy had an assignation with Celia, and therefore, he was the one who found her!"

"Perhaps you had better start at the beginning," said the viscount, perceiving that things were more complicated than he had hitherto supposed.

The twins proceeded with more haste than clarity to brief him on the previous evening's events. Mandy finished with a sigh and said, "That is why we came to you."

"Me?" objected Skippy starting to his feet once again, "how the devil am I to know what to do?"

The thought flitted through Mandy's mind that her delightful Skippy was not so all-knowing as her youth and inexperience had allowed her to think. However, there was no time for further speculation, for the butler once again made an appearance at the door of the morning room. "Squire Bevis and Mr. Alfred Speenham!" he announced.

Ned cursed under his breath. Mandy changed positions, almost instinctively taking a chair beside her brother. The viscount raised a brow, for he disliked both the squire and his son. He watched them enter the room and felt even less liking at their pomposity. The viscount put up his gold-rimmed quizzing-glass and scrutinized them, dropping it with a weary sigh, thus putting down whatever pretensions they had in mind.

Alfred Speenham, his hair more pomaded than usual, his beaklike nose seeming to have been polished, bent his head low over Mandy's reluctant hand. "Ah, Amanda, how well you do look, considering the ordeal your brother has put you through! I was quite unable to sleep last night."

"Really? Never say the demons of Bolton Abbey chased you home," said Mandy sweetly.

"I was not speaking of the plaguey things, but of poor Celia!" snapped Alfred, thinking his cousin had absolutely no sensitivity. He had no wish to court his sharp-tongued cousin, but there was nothing for it. His father had spoken.

Mandy observed her uncle. His balding head gleamed in the light as he turned his attention to Ned. His greeting had been formal, clipped; and she liked not his mien!

"Edward, it grieves me deeply, for it is a blot against the family, but I have come here to ask you to accompany me willingly to Harrowgate to speak with Magistrate Connors."

"Why?" inquired Mandy before Ned could speak. She didn't like this.

"Because he must. Your involvement in this case demands that you appear for questioning," said Squire Speenham.

Ned blushed, and Mandy got to her feet, clasping her hands together.

"Uncle . . . whatever does this mean?" she shrieked, quite frightened now.

"Please, Amanda, be seated. Do try and maintain a cool head," interposed Alfred with more gloating than concern for her welfare.

"Indeed, Amanda, my business is with Edward, and its nature is such that I may not discuss it—even with you," said her uncle, wiping his brow with a handkerchief.

"Indeed, Uncle!" snapped Amanda, mimicking his tone. "Whatever you have to discuss with Ned, you may discuss with us both. And he shall not go to Harrowgate with you—'tis inconvenient. So if you please, say whatever it is you obviously came to say."

Viscount Skippendon stepped forward at this juncture and added his voice to Mandy's words. "I must say, sir, that I find your behavior most objectionable. You saunter into *my home* with scarcely a by-your-leave . . . and yet think you can accost a guest of mine. Depend upon it, you are out there, sir!"

Squire Speenham turned to the viscount. "I do beg your pardon . . . it is just that this entire business is so distressing—and I would spare my nephew embarrassment before strangers."

"Skippy is not a stranger!" said Mandy putting up her chin.

"Nor do I have anything to be embarrassed about," added Ned sharply.

"I am afraid, young man, you are very much mistaken. Knew it . . . knew you would end in this manner with your gadding about . . . chin in the air . . . devil-may-care attitude," said the squire, pronouncing his judgment.

"Would you please put a halt to your rantings, Uncle, and advise us why you have come?" demanded his sister, showing as little respect as she felt.

"This morning . . . *this morning* . . . your Aunt Agatha found a page that was obviously torn from Celia's dairy. It had been ripped out and flung into her wastepaper basket . . . and it clearly states that your brother—your precious brother Edward—is the father of her unborn child!" announced Squire Speenham gleefully.

"I don't believe it," hissed Mandy.

"That is impossible!" shouted Ned. "I never . . . we never . . ."

"It is true, it is true!" said Alfred barely able to refrain from clapping his hands. "Edward brought down poor Celia!"

Mandy stepped forward and slapped his face, bringing a resounding silence to the room. He touched his red cheek, moving away from her, for the lady looked as though she might pursue this course of action further. However, Skippy stepped forward and gently took her arm.

"Calm yourself, Mandy. I'd as lief throw them out as not . . . shall I?"

"How can she have written such a thing . . . kindly allow me to see that page." Ned's face was white, his hand trembled with controlled anger.

"In good time, in good time. Now, Edward, you will kindly—and without any further delay—come with us," insisted his uncle.

"Oh, no, my man. Ned goes nowhere with you until I have seen that paper," said Skippy facing the older man squarely, his usually even temper quite ruffled.

Squire Bevis pulled out the wrinkled sheet from his coat pocket and slapped it into the viscount's waiting hand. "There! Though what right . . .?"

"May I remind you that you are *in my home*," said

Skippy, sternly interrupting him and casting his eyes over the crumpled page. His face was grim, and both Ned and Mandy flanked him as he read. Ned took up the page as the viscount raised his eyes to the squire.

"My dear sir, the poor girl writes that she intends to marry Edward and *make* him father of her child. She does *not* say that he *is* father of her child!"

"Oh, come now!" blustered the Squire, " 'tis there to be read. She is naming him as father."

"No, sir. Her exact words are: '. . . and Edward will be father to my child, and though he does not really love me now . . . . perhaps he shall . . . no matter.' Those are her words," finished Skippy, sneering, "Apparently the lady was capable of scheming!"

"Preposterous!" said Alfred, "Everyone knows she and Ned were meeting clandestinely. Why . . ."

"Be quiet, Alfred," said his father, noting that Mandy had moved in his direction. He retrieved the diary page and shook it at the viscount. "This is fact . . . you can't distort it with your theories." He turned to his nephew, "Now . . . must I call out the guards to fetch you, Edward? I had rather thought we might be spared a scene. Can you not come into Harrowgate like a man? There are questions which Magistrate Connors will have to put to you."

The viscount turned to Ned. "You had better go with him now. There is nothing for it, my friend. At any rate, you'll be home for dinner, and *I* will see Mandy home. Never fear, Ned. We'll see ourselves out of this tangle!"

"No!" snapped Mandy, "you can't mean to let them take him, Skip. Why . . . everyone will jump to conclusions. They will say he is guilty, and then we will be in for it!"

"I am certain your uncle will see to it that . . ." started Skip.

"No! *Uncle?* Not by blood, not by heart! He has never liked us. Oh, Skip, he is pleased to see Ned brought so low. Don't you see?"

"Hush, Mandy child. That is no way to speak of your uncle, and I am persuaded you do not. mean it. Your uncle has no wish to involve his own name in scandal . . ." tried Skip, for it would not do to antagonize Squire Speenham now. He had played it coolly with regard to the diary page's notation, but in truth, it could be damaging.

"Scandal?" repeated Mandy, cutting him short. "Don't you see that is why he has rushed here to take Ned . . . to protect his own name . . . so that no one will say he plays for his relatives. Everyone will say how good the squire is, taking in his own kin . . . against his heart. Ha!"

"No, Mandy, don't fret it," said Ned, placing a hand upon her shoulder. "I'll go with them and clear up the questions they have and, just as Skip says, I shall be home for dinner. And see to it that cook has a pheasant all trussed up the way I like it." He grinned, trying to bolster her spirits.

She clung to him suddenly and, when Alfred put his hand on Ned's shoulder, he whirled on him viciously. "Get your filthy paws off me, you blackguard!" Again Alfred stepped warily back and waited until Ned bade his sister be calm and then led the way out.

Mandy went to the window and watched them ride off before turning on the viscount. "You shouldn't have allowed uncle to take him off. He won't be back, Skip. I just know they won't release him."

"Hush now, girl, there was nothing for it. Take up a seat and keep yourself quiet for a moment or two. Must do something . . . now!" said the viscount going to his writing desk.

"What are you doing?" she asked from a troubled countenance.

"Writing your guardian," said Skippy with determination.

"That old thing? What can he do?" asked she with disdain.

"Old?" said Skip with surprise. The Duke of Margate, one of his closest cronies, was scarcely a year older than himself, and he had never thought of himself as an *old thing*. "He is not old, and he is a most powerful figure. He could do something—if I can bestir him to it!"

"He hasn't bothered with us in this entire past year—why should he now?"

"Because he won't like the scandal," replied Skippy frankly.

"Indeed! He sounds a most selfish creature."

Skippy wasted no time disputing this. He was fond of his rakehell friend and, although the Duke was possessed of many sterling qualities, one could not deny that he was indeed self-centered.

"Oh, Skip, whatever can we do? We must do something, yet I feel so helpless."

The viscount sealed his hastily written epistle and rose to his feet.

"We will get the duke. He'll know the way out of this muddle, see if he don't!"

Chapter Four

Brock Haydon, eighth Duke of Margate, tooled his high-stepping black stallion through the London hubbub with deft skill. A cart filled with vegetables had lost a wheel, spilling both owner and contents. Several vehicles of various sizes and classes were held up while the little man gathered up his source of livelihood. Curses born of impatience were flung at the farmer's head, but he shook his dirty fists in response and deliberately slowed the process of gathering his wares. However, though the farmer, the lopsided vegetable cart, and the stalled traffic were very much in the weary duke's path, they but momentarily slowed his way. He had had a long hot ride from Brighton, and he wanted refreshment and a bath to banish the fatigue of the day. As the Duke was accustomed to getting his wishes, he merely urged his horse up onto the curbing, ignoring the protests of pedestrians, until he had circumvented the fuss in the street.

A few moments later he was dismounting before a fashionable town house situated at the corner of Berkeley Square and giving up his steed to his waiting ostler. "I want Prancer rubbed down well, lad, and have that left fore shoe replaced."

"Ay, Yer Grace," said the young urchin, smiling at the coin the duke placed in his hand. The wild young duke might be a flash cove full of orders but he surely was a generous one, thought the boy, leading the prime blood away.

The duke brushed the dust away from his summer-weight blue riding coat as he mounted the steps and smiled broadly to see his door open wide before he could reach the knocker. Apparently, his butler had been on the look-out for him, he thought with amusement as he dropped his top hat and gloves into the man's hand and sauntered into the bright central hall. He paused before an oval stainwood table.

"Hello, Graves, hot enough for you?" greeted the duke amicably.

"Indeed, yes, Your Grace, I hope you did not find your ride too tiring," answered the old retainer politely. He had been the family butler for close onto twenty years and had watched the young man before him grow from a noisy but lovable boy into the proud, disdainful, and often bored holder of the title.

"Any mail of importance while I was away?" asked

the duke carelessly, moving toward the white double doors.

"Yes, Your Grace. A letter came by Special Service two weeks ago, and I have been in a quandary with regard to it ever since," said the butler.

"Oh?" The duke raised one black straight brow.

"Indeed, Your Grace, 'twas marked 'Urgent' on the envelope, and I thought to forward it on to you at Brighton until I received your note that you would be home shortly, and then . . ."

"And then I never arrived. Sorry, old boy. I was detained . . . unavoidably, by a chance meeting with an . . . old friend," said the duke, smiling at the memory of the pleasant week he had spent with a most beguiling damsel.

"The letter is from Wharfedale Manor, Your Grace, and sits atop a pile of correspondence on your desk in the library," offered the butler, secretly thinking that his master's lackadaisical attitude did not become his position. " 'Tis from the Viscount Skippendon."

"Skippy? By Jove, man, why didn't you say so at once?" The duke's coldly handsome features lighted up almost boyishly. "Haven't had a word from that dratted fellow in over two months . . . the dog!" He completed the distance to the white double doors, flung them open, and descended on his desk with some force. There he found Skippy's letter, broke open the seal, and sat down upon the Regency chair to peruse its contents.

Margate:
To get to the point, you may recall that you are the guardian for the Sherborne twins, poor souls! As it happens they are friends of mine, have been for some

years past. At any rate, better get yourself up here
at once, for they have managed to embroil themselves
in murder and, demmit, Brock, it don't look good!

Yours,
Skip

The duke knuckled his eyes before re-reading this
astounding missive, sure that his first perusal of its
contents could not have been accurate. However, this
hope was soon laid to rest, as a second and third reading dispelled all astonishment. The duke proceeded to
swear with such lucidity and vitality that when Graves
appeared with a tray of refreshment, the butler opened
his eyes wide and hoped that the duke's aunt (with all
her retinue of servants) was not about to descend upon
them.

He received a curt thank-you and an order to have
a bath prepared before he escaped the duke's notice,
then hurriedly departed to convey the duke's wishes to
the lackeys. While His Grace's servants went about
seeing to his needs, the duke sat thoughtfully pulling
his sensuous lower lip, studying his friend's letter
gravely. He sighed wearily, for it was true—and quite
embarrassing as well. To be guardian over a pair but
seven years younger than he, was not a comfortable
situation for a young man portraying himself to the
haut ton as a fashionable rake. He had found himself
saddled with the Sherborne twins when his father died
nine months ago leaving him the title, the Margate
wealth, and these Yorkshire wards.

He chose to ignore them. After all, he reasoned,
they were not children in need of attention, and they
would soon come of age and be their own masters.
Therefore, he gave over their estates into his capable

solicitor's hands and, though he mourned his father's passing, it had been expected and something he was quite capable of dealing with. Before long he had returned to the unworthy pursuits that had often called down his father's rebukes, but truth was he was sick of everything and everyone except a few intimates like Skippy—or the Beau who was no longer about to win or bestow a smile.

Recently, very recently, the duke's eyes began straying to Parliament. There were causes to be fought that caught his interest. There was home rule for Ireland, there were issues that touched his heart, and he knew he wanted to take his seat and make that seat powerful. Therefore, this was no time for his name to be dragged through scandal. Evidently the twins, though nearly grown, had managed to play with the devil, and the fact that he was their guardian was bound to make a juicy moiety for the gossipmongers. He frowned over the thought. He didn't like that. He had always managed to gain the things he wanted, for in addition to his self-assurance, his arrogance, his title, his money, and his extraordinary good looks, he was a fighter. Hell and damnation! He'd go up to the Sherborne estate and take those absurd twins in hand. Murder be damned!

In the last three weeks things had gone quite badly at Sherborne. As Mandy had feared, Ned had not been allowed to return. He had been questioned thoroughly by the Harrowgate magistrate, who had decided to hold him in the single cell at Harrowgate Court Hall until a judge could be brought in for a hearing. By the next morning word spread through the neighboring villages that Lord Sherborne had murdered his poor lovely cousin. Only the few who knew him well doubted it, for he was subject to all the prejudices the indigent have for the·wealthy. Bitterness was rife amongst the townspeople, and Mandy, riding her horse through Harrowgate toward the Court Hall heard, "Blackguard is wot he is! Bedded his own cousin, he did, and stubbled her without no one sayin' him nay. Well now, the covey is twigged, and he'll hang, he will, just like the black'earted cull he be!"

Mandy wanted to cry and when she visited Ned in his bleak cell she wanted to scream. Her concern grew with each day, and more than one person pointed her out, brazenly saying within her hearing, "Queer, ain't it? 'Ow they be twins . . . their phizzes so alike . . . she 'ave the look of an angel . . . and he the 'eart of a divil!"

She stomped into the stable and went into Chauncy's broad burly arms. He had been her groom for eighteen years, and she and Ned had already trusted him with their lives more than once. "Oh Chauncy . . ." she cried shielding her dark eyes with her bare hand, "the inquest is on the morrow, and I fear . . . oh, Chauncy, it won't go in his favor. I just know it . . ."

He was a large man with a wide round jaw and penetrating brown eyes. He wagged his finger at her, "Lordy, Miss Mandy, jest look at ye carrying on like some wilted bloom. That ain't how I taught ye. Why, ye shame me, ye do!"

She laughed uneasily and dropped into a pile of straw, accustomed as she was to the scent of the stables. "But Chauncy, it doesn't augur well for Ned. Those who don't know him are sure he did it. And those who do . . . can't explain away the dreadful circumstances of it all. Even Sir Owen who believes Ned and wants to help . . . doesn't know how to prove him innocent."

"Never you mind that now, missy. He'll come through this ken right and tight, see if he don't," said the man, rubbing his smooth chin thoughtfully. "What we got to do is find that Elly girl—and that diary of Miss Celia's—there be the thing of it!"

Suddenly a young livery boy came bowling into the stables, his face lit up with excitement. "Chauncy," he exclaimed, "it's finished for the young lord!" He spied Miss Mandy hugging her knees in the straw pile and pulled himself up short, casting his eyes groundward.

"Speak up, lad!" ordered Chauncy rounding on him, "What's that you say?"

"It's Mrs. Brinley . . . she come forward . . . said she didn't want to but felt it was her duty. That's wot she said . . ." mumbled the urchin, blushing before Mandy's inquiring gaze.

"Duty? What do you mean, boy?" urged Mandy, getting to her feet and shaking out her blue print muslin.

"Said to Magistrate Connors that 'er stepdaughter dun opened 'er mummer to 'er 'ow His Lordship meant to cry off . . . and 'ow she . . . Miss Celia 'ad the way of it to force his 'and."

"That be a whisker!" cried Chauncy, raising his hand.

"I ain't cuttin' a wheedle . . . 'onest Chauncy . . . had it from that snirp wot brings His Lordship his vittles."

Mandy's face paled. "How could Aunt Agatha do such a thing? How could she? And why did she wait until now?"

"Out wit ye," roared Chauncy at the boy who rushed to do this bidding. He turned to his mistress, "I don't like the sound of things, missy. It do look bad. I was hoping we'd have time to get our 'ands on that diary, but we can't leave His Lordship to the dogs. No, not with the scales weighted agin him."

"Then we proceed as we discussed yesterday?" said Mandy, her eyes brightening.

"Aye, I don't like it none, for I don't take to floutin' the law. But those twiddlepoops in Harrowgate wot thinks they be the law leave us no choice in the thing . . . do they?"

"Indeed they do not, Chauncy. But . . . this means we shall be fugitives. Oh, Chauncy, I don't like putting you in such a way," said Mandy frowning.

"Coo, missy . . . as though sech as that would be more than a brace o' snaps!" said Chauncy, settling the matter.

Ned fidgeted in his dreary cell. He had received one visit from his sister that morning and another in the late afternoon. He was ready, anxious, and restless. He listened to the clip-clop of horses on the cobblestone street and to the laughter of farmers and cits as they made their way to a near-by tavern . . . and waited.

Amanda Sherborne's pretty white muslin gown was hiked up to enable her to ride astride. Her golden locks were dressed provocatively upon her head, and little white ribbon bows above her ears gave her the appearance of an adorable and innocent young miss. Chauncy sat silently astride his big roan, holding the reins of another horse at his back. It was dark when they arrived at Harrowgate and made their way to the Court Hall. A dim light showed through a first-floor window, and Mandy cast her eyes about nervously as she dismounted and tethered her horse. Chauncy followed silently to the single wooden door and pushed it open for her to enter.

A dark-haired, heavyset yeoman in white shirt-sleeves sat behind the desk, his feet stretched out and crossed before him, his head resting sleepily on his shoulder. Mandy cleared her throat prettily, bringing him to a sense of awareness.

"Eh . . . eh?" he said, sitting up suddenly and focusing on the vison before him. He was the night guard and therefore had never seen Amanda before. "Who be ye . . .?"

"I am so sorry," drawled the lady, smiling sweetly. "I do so dislike having to bother you, sir."

The yeoman had by this time discovered that the vision was real and was addressing him in a manner few women, let alone one with such a smile, had ever done. He responded warmly. "Bother? 'Tis no bother, ma'am . . ."

"I'm so glad. I am Amanda Sherborne, and I should like to visit with my brother . . . His Lordship. He is a guest here, you see," she said, still smiling.

He sighed sorrowfully, unhappy to have to deliver a negative reply so early in their acquaintance. "I am afraid that is not possible."

"But . . . why?"

" 'Tis the rules, Miss Sherborne. No visitors are permitted in the evening."

"Now, who is to know?" she asked putting a coy finger to his protruding chin.

He grinned ingenuously. "I can't break the rules . . ."

She allowed her finger to trace the outline of his thick mustache.

"Rules are monstrously provoking . . . and I just want to see my brother for a moment. You see we are twins . . . and I had this odious dream that he had been beaten. My mind just won't rest easy until I have seen him," she said, pouting prettily.

He cast his eyes about. "Well, actually . . . there is no one about to know . . . if you promise not to stay above a minute."

"You sweet creature . . . I could just kiss you," cried Amanda as she watched him fumble for the keys.

He turned to Chauncy, "You'll have to wait for your mistress here."

Chauncy nodded, and Amanda went along with the yeoman down the long corridor to a small oak door. As the man worked the key and brought up his head, he found a horse pistol pointing at him. It had been well concealed under Mandy's shawl, for she and Chauncy had anticipated his having to remain in the outer room. As the yeoman opened his mouth to scream for help, he felt a strong hand come from behind and silence him, for Chauncy had timed it well.

The yeoman was persuaded to sit in a chair where he was gagged, tied, and blindfolded, and consequently left in place of Lord Sherborne. The summer night was sweet as three riders piked off and headed for Bolton

Abbey ruins. There a room Ned and Mandy had discovered as children had been prepared for their visit, and there they planned to stay, depending on ghosts and demons to frighten off any would-be intruders. It would be their base from which they could search for Elly Bonner and Celia's missing diary.

Chapter Five

_____

The duke had elected to ride in comfort to Wharfedale Manor. He rode in his sleek carriage, his baggage loaded above, his valet seated before him, and Prancer tethered to the rear. He had started out the very next morning from London and was now on the last leg of his three-day journey. But there had been delays. First, the front wheels were damaged. Then they had been delayed again when that same wheel wobbled and would have certainly fallen off and sent them into the ditch had not the duke realized something was wrong and called his driver to a halt. Again the wheel was temporarily repaired and they were able to continue the journey to Skippy's estate.

The duke's thoughts were a jumble; his black wavy

hair was in some disorder from the various unexpected vicissitudes of the journey, and his temper sharply put out at having to leave London as soon as he had returned. However, some of his ruffled feelings were soothed upon the reunion with Skippy. They jostled one another for a few moments, threw questions and answers regarding several of their mutual friends, and then settled down to imbibe some excellent brandy. The duke was given all the pertinent facts regarding the Sherborne twins, Mandy's rescue of her brother, and their subsequent disappearance two weeks previously.

"Never say so!" ejaculated the duke with mixed astonishment and interest. "What sort of girl is this Amanda? She behaves a veritable hoyden . . . breaking her brother out of custody indeed! Damn! Don't they realize this makes it all the worse for him?"

"Not really, Brock," said Skippy gravely. "Thing is . . . what with their aunt coming forward with that latest piece of nonsense . . . it looked very bad for Ned. Couldn't look any more guilty than he already did. Leaning over the body he was, when Owen found him . . . then as if that wasn't enough, their aunt found that page from the missing diary, practically naming him as father—or at least appearing to do so—and then . . . his aunt coming forward and saying Celia had the notion to force him to marry her when he didn't wish to. Looks bad for the lad."

"Indeed it does," commented the duke gravely. "Could he—in your opinion—could he have fathered her child and killed her—this Celia?"

"Never!" said Skippy.

"Then who could have done the thing?"

"Demme, Brock! That's the thing . . . had a string of admirers . . . and she was well able to keep mum

about them. No one knows who got close enough—
except that maid of hers. But she and the diary have
vanished."

"Odd circumstance that, don't you think? I mean if
the father of Miss Brinley's child murdered her, why
would the girl's maid run off with the diary? It doesn't
make sense."

"Eh . . . don't know. The whole thing don't make
sense if you ask me."

"Well, nothing for it, Skip. I shall go up to Sherborne
Halls and speak with Mrs. Brinley. I mean to get at
this, my man, mark me!"

Skippy regarded his friend thoughtfully. "Never
doubted it, Brock."

"Have your man call your carriage out for me, will
you? Mine is done up."

"What? Going up to the Halls at this time? Good
God! You've been traveling all day."

"The sooner I solve this thing . . . the sooner I
escape Yorkshire. Can't figure what's kept *you* up
here so long. Can't be the heather, John, for it didn't
come into bloom until summer, and you've been up
here . . . what? Good Lord! Six months at least!
Why?"

"I'll go ring for my carriage to be brought round,"
said Skippy, ignoring this question.

The duke looked inquisitively at his friend's countenance but could find there only acute discomfort.
Odd—in all the years they had been cronies he had
never known Skippy to be secretive. This was certainly
something new—and most curious!

Some twenty minutes later the duke stood, his hands
clasped behind his dark blue coat, his feet apart, his

blue eyes thoughtful, as he gazed up at the portrait of
the Sherborne twins. This had been done for their
eighteenth birthday and hung magnificently between
two large bookcases in the Sherborne library. Their
coloring and similarity he found most striking, but it
was Mandy's likeness that captivated his attention.
What sort of female was this? Surely no angel—not
with those wild dark eyes—and how came she to have
such dark eyes when her hair was the color of gold? He
had known many ladies, but none of them would have
led her groom into a jail and held a pistol to a yeoman's
head in order to release a prisoner. This facet of
Mandy's personality intrigued him, and now her portrait tantalized him.

It was her eyes! The artist had captured a glimmer of
secret amusement—as though the owner found life
ludicrous. The duke himself often thought so, but
whereas he was wearied by life's absurdities, she appeared to be entertained.

Mrs. Brinley entered the room in a flutter and broke
his musings with resounding force. She was a dark
woman of large proportions and little grace—and there
was something about her that he did not like. When she
opened her mouth, he found his distaste increased.

Finding a superior male with as much address as
charm, Mrs. Brinley bustled and gushed, "Your Grace
. . . how utterly delightful. If only you had sent word
. . . I would have prepared a room to receive you. But
no matter . . . one can be made ready in a trice. Our
servants need do no more than place a hot brick in your
bed as I have them air out all the rooms whether they
are in use or not . . ."

He put up an imperative hand.

"Do not concern yourself, madam. I do not stay, for I am promised to the Viscount Skippendon." Then, deciding to plunge right in, "Of course, you realize why I am here."

"Indeed. It is such a dreadful business. My poor lovely Celia . . . seduced . . . murdered! Oh! I am heartsick over the entire wretched affair!" said Mrs. Brinley, putting a plump hand to her heart as though to steady its beating.

The duke watched her carefully, looked into her light brown eyes and found there—fear. Odd, he thought. Again he plunged into the heart of the matter. "I understand that your stepdaughter was three months with child. Was not your nephew at Cambridge three months ago?"

"Well, yes, but he had been home for a fortnight. For the Easter holidays, you know . . ." she offered hesitantly.

He wondered what she had to gain by Ned's hanging for the murder of her stepdaughter. He found himself siding with the golden-haired lad almost instinctively. "Then it is your firm belief that Lord Sherborne seduced your daughter at that time?"

"I simply don't know. I only know that he allowed his eyes to follow her about . . . and I often heard him throw her a pretty line."

"I see," he said gravely, causing a nervous flutter to pinch through Mrs. Agatha Brinley. "May I know whether or not a proper search has been instituted for your stepdaughter's diary."

"Of course, but it has not been found," she answered hastily.

"Odd—that one page should be torn out, I mean."

"My maid found it and brought it to me. But the diary vanished . . . as did Elly Bonner, Celia's maid."

"Would you be so kind as to call your maid here. I should like to speak with her."

"About what?" asked Agatha Brinley nervously.

."You shall see," said the duke putting up a brow.

She rose and went to the hall, calling the butler and asking him to fetch her maid. She pulled at the skirt of her buff-colored muslin and fidgeted about before resuming her seat some moments later. A frightened young woman some thirty years of age, with a mobcap and full white apron over a gray dress bobbed into the room and dropped a curtsy.

The duke smiled warmly at her in an attempt to put her at ease.

"What is your name, child?" he asked gently.

"Sally, Yer Grace."

"Sally, I have a few questions. Please don't be frightened . . . and do your best to answer them as accurately as you can."

"Yes, Yer Grace."

"Did you know Elly Bonner?"

"Jest to pass the time of day, sir. 'Twas I that brought her to Miss Celia's notice when Miss Celia said 'tweren't convenient to be sharing a maid with her stepmama. Met Elly in town one day . . . and we got jest a bit friendly . . . told her there might be a post for her. She come . . . she got the job. But we was never close."

"Did she ever mention her family to you? Where they might live?"

"No. Wait, there . . . she did onct say she had a beau . . . and how they would one day marry and live as high as quality . . ."

"Did she mention where this suitor of hers resided? How he made his living?"

"No, Yer Grace . . . and I've always had a notion it wasn't pound dealing that was his ken . . . no . . . not from all I gleaned from her."

"Did you never see him then? He didn't come calling for her here at the Halls?"

"Bless me, no! Always thought 'twas strange the way she would take off in the middle of the night. She did, you know, though Miss Celia never suspicioned it. She was takin' off to meet wit him, she was! But onct, when I went in for Mrs. Brinley to Wharfedale village—for some errand or other—she asked if she could come along. She loped off . . . and I was near fair to tearing m'hair out, I was, when she didn't get back till dark. Don't take to driving the cart after the sun sets." She tilted her head thoughtfully. "Maybe he had a place near the village . . . can't say fer certain though."

"Thank you, Sally, you have been most helpful indeed," said the duke. She bobbed herself out of the room, and the duke watched her leave before turning back to Mrs. Brinley who, he noted with interest, was looking more than a little irritated. Again he wondered what she stood to gain by the young lord's destruction?

"Hang me, Mandy . . . I'm stalled and near to milling!" expostulated Edward Sherborne testily, shifting position on his linen-covered straw bed. "We've been here two weeks and are no closer to finding Elly Bonner than we were when I was being held in the court jail. And demme! These tallow candles give off a fiendish odor in these closed quarters!"

"Confound it, Ned, it isn't as though we have the favor of free movement to aid us," snapped his sister, for she was just as despondent and irritable. "And lud! they do have a vile scent . . . never noticed it before."

"That's 'cause we always used wax before. Whatever possessed you to gather tallow? Blister it, girl! Tallow's made from animal fat!"

"I took what I could find without arousing suspicion, Ned . . . and I must say it is not very handsome of you . . . blaming me for such nonsense." She stopped and looked away, just a little hurt.

Ned, Mandy, and Chauncy were fugitives, and the immediate future offered no alternative. "Odds fish, Mandy, I don't mean to croak at you, but demme if I see a way out of this tangle. And now you and Chauncy are drawn into it."

"Hush, Neddy. We will muddle through somehow. We must!"

Chauncy lowered his head and entered the arched doorway of the dimly lit underground chamber. He broke into a smile and he held out in one hand two ripe peaches. Ned and Mandy lost no time in reaching for the proffered treat and quickly bit into the tasty fruit.

"However did you get these?" cried Mandy joyously, for they had not been eating well these last few days.

"Not everyone at the Halls has turned their backs on us, loveys. Yer aunt . . . she ogles the kitchen, she does, so as cook 'ad a time of it twigging this 'ere," He swung a basket from behind his back and laid it at their feet. "The peaches bein' the easiest to pass behind yer aunt's phiz!"

"But why is Aunt watching the kitchen? Do you think she would actually try to stop food from being taken to us?" said Mandy in surprise.

"It queers me to know why, but I 'ave it plain as pikestaff that be jest wot she be trying her famble at," answered Chauncy, opening the basket and producing a well cooked chicken.

This was immediately pounced upon and, as all three sat back to enjoy the meal, Chauncy felt satisfied enough to remove the Bullycock hat he was rarely seen without and sighed gustily over the drumstick in his hand. Then remembering that he had something to tell them, he shook the drumstick at the twins and said quietly as though he were about to drop an egg, "Got a piece of news. There be a tallow-faced stranger staying at the Cock Pit in Harrowgate."

Ned did not feel this was of sufficient import to gaze up from the chicken breast he was zestfully devouring. However, his sister brought her dark eyes up to Chauncy's large face.

"Why should that matter to us?"

"Yes, they say he be tallow-faced and with a pair of cat-sticks for legs. But a wisty cove at that," continued Chauncy, appraising the drumstick bone for any chance meat he might have missed.

"Oh, please, Chauncy, don't be so provoking! What is this strange creature's connection to us?" asked Mandy. Ned's head came up, for he was made curious by the tone of her voice.

"Brett—he says the fellow claims to be on 'oliday—but Brett—you know Brett, don't you, my lord?"

"Eh . . . you mean the Cock Pit's owner. Indeed I do. Capital fellow," grinned Ned, pleased to find some meaning to this conversation.

"That's the one. Ay . . . Brett don't talk idly . . . and he don't believe Mr. Fowler be 'ere on 'oliday. Asks a lot of questions . . . thinks Fowler be cutting a rare wheedle. Got a strong notion m'self that Fowler be a Bow Street runner!" said Channcy, finally letting go.

Ned jumped to his feet. "May the devil take the fellow . . . for if *he* don't, we are done for!"

"Oh, Chauncy . . . a Bow Street runner . . . never say they have called a runner all the way from London . . . just to hunt us out?" cried Mandy in dismay. "Why, if that is so, he is bound to check over these ruins."

"Listen to the pair of you. Why it shames me, it does, to see the light of m'old eyes carrying on like sucklings! Coo . . . if he be a runner—and I think it likely—'twill be famous good sport tipping him the double. But we be wasting time. Now that ye ate yer best, get ready to shake off some of yer restiness," said the groom portentously.

"Why . . . what's afoot?" asked Ned.

"Twigged the viscount's coach going up to the Halls. Should soon be finished with whatever business he has up there."

"What?" ejaculated Ned and his sister in unison.

"Why would Skippy go up to the Halls?" asked Mandy, drawing her brows together.

"It queers me to tell ye, lovey . . . seeing as I didn't stop to pass the time of day wit His Lordship. But if ye means to find out, best get that bandanna over those bright yella curls and go stretch yer 'orses legs," said Chauncy seating himself on the bench. Mandy had long ago exchanged her pretty muslin for a white linen shirt, buckskin breeches, and an ill-fitting riding coat. She now wrapped a black bandanna round her head and tucked in her long tresses before pulling on a bullycock hat her groom had managed to acquire for her. Ned glanced over her, laughed as he always did whenever they went out so attired, and picked up their pistols, putting one into her hand. They made their way down the narrow tunnel to a set of worn stone steps that took them to a wooden trap door above their heads. This opened into a dark stone-walled room, one of the few that still boasted a ceiling and door. Here they kept their horses which they now quickly saddled. As Mandy felt the warm summer night air stroke her cheeks, she laughed.

"Oh, Neddy, it's good to be out of that dungeon—oh, Lud, it's good!"

"I'm prime for a bit of sport myself," agreed her brother.

A notion struck her. "Neddy, let's have a bit of fun with Skip."

"Eh . . . how?" asked her brother hopefully.

"I'd say we look every bit the high tobys."

He burst out laughing, "You look a snip! High toby indeed! There isn't a fool alive that would take you for a bridle cull . . ."

Mandy felt this to be monstrously insulting and put her chin in the air. "Stubble it, covey! I can pass thieves' cant as well as any and a sight better than you. And as to my size . . . this . . . " she said, patting the horse pistol in its saddle holster, "should make up for the difference."

Ned eyed her not without admiration. She was game, Mandy was . . . always had been . . . no society miss . . . but pluck to the backbone.

"Done, m'girl!"

They passed through the glen to the Abbey road,

taking up strategic positions and hoping that the viscount had not already passed. They whiled away the time flinging thieves' cant at one another and laughing at the reflection they presented to each other with scarfs pulled up to their eyes. "High toby—Ha!" chuckled Ned. "You look like a scrawny, bright-eyed gamine!"

"Hush now! I heard horses," urged Mandy from across the road.

As the viscount's coach lumbered round the curve in the road and approached the clump of woods bordering on either side, Mandy could hear the viscount's driver whistling. She motioned with a wave to her brother and rushed out, gun in hand. The carriage slowed to a complete stop before its two assailants. Ned, noting that the driver was reaching for something at his side, suddenly realized that their little hoax could be dangerous.

"Put your fambles to the sky, m'buck!" said he in ominous tones. "That's the way of it. Now I'll take your barking iron!" he said, reaching out to receive this, at the same time keeping the fellow covered with his own unloaded gun.

Well pleased with the results of this first effort, Mandy urged her horse gently forward to the coach door, surprised that the viscount had chosen to remain in his carriage. She had expected Skippy to come jumping out, shouting curses at their heads, for he had often expatiated on the evils of highwaymen. She leaned over her horse and knocked at the carriage door with her foot. "Well now, m'fine covey! Out with ye!" she ordered in a deep voice.

No one appeared, and Mandy glanced towards her brother. He shrugged his shoulders in response, and once again Mandy was staring through the darkness at the carriage door. "Eh . . . be ye asleep, covey? I said out wit ye—before I let some of that fine quality blood of yers. Come on . . . ye've been snabbled. Out wit ye! Let's 'ave a lookee at yer phiz."

Ned was admiring his sister's command of the thieves' cant when his brow went up with surprise. The carriage door did indeed open to his sister's authoritative tune, but the male who descended from its confines could not possibly be the viscount. From where Ned managed his steed, the man dropping nimbly out of the coach certainly appeared taller, more powerfully built, darker—and blister it!—Ned got a look at the man's face—and he was *not* the viscount.

However, the carriage door had opened into Mandy's horse, and she found that she had to maneuver her steed out of its way. Thus, it was that she did not encounter this startling realization at the same moment as her brother. She steadied her horse into position and ordered the fellow whom she thought to be Skippy, "Stand and deliver, gent!"

The duke's eyes glittered dangerously in the moonlight as he brought his ruggedly handsome countenance up with an angry jerk. It was at this moment that Mandy perceived what her brother was trying desperately to tell her by his frantic movements! Her eyes focused on the duke's visage and, while she found there an incredibly attractive male who would have at any other time and any other place certainly caused the lady's heart to flutter, his powerful form now filled her with dismay. She was unaware that the gentleman held a pistol concealed in the folds of his cape and that the last time the duke had leveled his pistol at a high toby, the man had bought a bullet through the heart. The duke's hard eyes found the bridle cull's youthful face nearly half concealed in the folds of a dark scarf. He scanned the youth quickly, but all he could determine was that this particular highwayman was unusually young—far too young to go the way of his predecessor. Hence, his trigger finger relaxed, and he frowned up at the youth.

"Rather lean in years to be riding the road, my cull," said the duke casually, keeping a wary eye on the toby at the head of his coach and moving imperceptibly, putting Mandy's horse between himself and her accomplice.

"Who . . . who . . . are you?" breathed Mandy, struck dumb at finding that though 'twas Skippy's coach and Skippy's driver, 'twas *not* Skippy standing before her!

"By Jupiter, you are a cool one!" said the duke, somewhat surprised by her unusual question. "Do you always insist on an introduction before you relieve your victims of their blunt?"

"Stubble it, gent!" growled Mandy, finding her voice and bravely asserting herself in the vernacular. "Come on," called Mandy to her brother. "Let's pike off. I've no fancy to prig this big un's pockets."

The duke found this alteration in the highwayman's plans rather more than astounding and looked from one toby to the other in open wonder as he heard Ned heartily agree.

"Ay, then, so be it!" called Ned, eager to be off. He threw the driver's barking iron into the bushes flanking the road. "You can fetch your iron when we've loped off."

Odd, thought the duke, what sort of highwaymen were they?

"Not so fast, my little cull! It wouldn't be polite to lope off just yet," he said, exhibiting his own gun.

The moonlight glittered wickedly on the black metal, and Mandy's eyes opened wide with fright. This was turning out to be the devil's own affair. She spoke with more courage than she felt.

"If ye 'ave a mind to twig our rig, ye'll 'ave to tap m'claret 'ere and now wit that prime barking iron of yers—for I 'ave it in mind to leave ye at peace—and square it right and tight." She attempted to move her horse away as she spoke, but he anticipated her and, reaching out, caught her snapple rein. Suddenly she felt herself roughly and speedily yanked out of her saddle. She felt the gentleman's viselike grip go round her waist, sure he had arms that were not fashioned of blood and bone. She kicked and hit at his body, but this was no man but a thing of steel.

As she struggled, wriggled, and flung abuse at her subjugator's head, it became stunningly apparent to the duke that the youth he held captive was no male. His eyes opened to their fullest as he spun her forcibly round by her dainty shoulders to peer at her piquant if somewhat soiled countenance.

"Fiend seize it!" hissed His Grace, exploding with agitation. "Stand a moment, you undersized fury!"

By this time Ned had left off guarding the driver and had jumped to the ground rushing the duke with greater intention than effectiveness. He grabbed one of the duke's powerful shoulders and cried impressively, "Blackguard! If you have a mind to fight, then meet *me,* swine, for *I* am more your size!"

The duke released Mandy with slow, cool calm. His mien sent a shiver through her. Even before he had brought up his shattering fist, Mandy knew what would happen. Ned was landed a settler that sent him sprawling backwards onto the earth, and his sister unthinkingly shrieked his name as she rushed to his side. His bullycock hat had gone flying and hers joined it as she bent over to aid him into a sitting position. The duke watched this with considerable interest and his sharp eyes lit upon one stray golden curl peeping out of Mandy's black bandanna at the nape of her neck. Suddenly, the entire thing made total sense to him.

Ned was rubbing his chin ruefully as Mandy planted their hats upon their heads.

"Caught me on the bonebox . . . but don't get hipped . . . I'm all right," he was assuring his sister. They glared at the duke, but suddenly he was ignoring them and walking to the driver's box where Skippy's driver sat watching open-mouthed. With the duke's realization came the decision to send off the groom who was unknown to him and therefore not yet to be trusted. He spoke to the curious man in the box seat.

"I've got these two devils in hand. You may return to the Manor and advise the viscount that I shall come along much later this evening. He needn't wait up for me."

"But . . ." began the fellow.

"I did not propose a discussion of the matter," said the duke coldly. "Now kindly follow my instructions."

"Yes, Yer grace," replied the driver, thinking the duke queer in the attic—but then there was no telling what the Quality would do.

As the coach rumbled on down the Abbey road,

the duke turned, folded his left arm across his chest so that he rested his right elbow upon it, and rubbed his mouth. He watched as Mandy brushed the dust off Ned's clothing and soothed her brother's injured pride. The scarf no longer covered her mouth but had fallen around her neck. She raised her face and her dark eyes were bright with undisguised anger as she met the duke's, "You are a wretched, odious brute! We didn't take anything from you and wanted nothing more than to be allowed to proceed on our way."

"My! The vixen can actually speak without the aid of thieves' cant," taunted the duke. "Allow you to proceed on your way? No doubt to detain a less formidable traveler."

"Why you . . . you . . . " started Mandy, glaring.

"Tch, tch, ill-mannered creature," said the duke, his tone perfectly amiable. "It would seem my previous laxity with regard to your supervision has not borne good fruit."

"I have no notion of what you are speaking, but you are . . ." began Mandy.

Her brother interrupted. "Never mind that." He turned to the duke. "Look here . . . you have no right to keep us . . . we took nothing from you."

"You took time from me," answered the duke sternly. "You accosted my driver on a public road and aimed a gun at his head—not to mention mine!"

"It wasn't loaded," snapped Mandy, wondering who the deuce this arrogant fellow was.

"Ah! But he, poor fellow, had no way of knowing that and suffered all the trials a man undergoes when he thinks he might be shot at any moment. And for what? A lark!" said the duke in a scathing voice.

Mandy bit her lip; her brother opened his eyes wide. How did this self-assured man—and one Ned was beginning to realize was not of an ordinary stamp—how did he realize they were on a lark?

"You play an odd game, sir. But we are not mice and, I assure you, will not scurry about waiting your intentions!" said Mandy, her chin in the air.

"Yes," agreed her brother. "Who the devil are you?"

The duke grinned. "That particular question plagues you. Whom were you expecting?"

"Confound you!" said Mandy in very unladylike tones. "Whom do you think, but the Viscount Skippendon. And as you know already, 'twas for sport as we are friends of his. And he, I assure you, would not have minded in the least! Now, if you will stand out of the way, we shall not trouble you further."

He barred her path, and their eyes met in battle. She felt a flush steal over her even in the darkness and glanced away. He chuckled.

"You may have noticed—Miss Sherborne—that I dismissed my conveyance!"

Mandy gasped, her brother dropped his jaw, and both waited for him to say more, unable themselves to say a word. His eyes took in their terror, and he realized suddenly that they were undergoing a very real, a very acute discomfort, and he took pity on them. "You may—both of you—relax. I am not going to do either of you harm. Indeed, I came to your heathenish moors for the express purpose of extricating you from the difficulties you have managed to plunge yourselves into!"

"Who . . . who . . . are you?" breathed Mandy, clasping and unclasping her hands, for in spite of his assurance she was nervous and strangely agitated.

He inclined his head slightly. "Have you not guessed? I would have credited you with more intelligence!" He bowed gracefully. "You have the pleasure of making the acquaintance of your guardian, Brock Haydon, Duke of Margate."

"You lie," hissed Mandy. "Our guardian is a gouty old man."

The duke's brow went up in surprise. "I have no idea where you received such an account of me. But I do assure you that I have never suffered from the gout . . . nor have I been thought old—though I certainly have some six or seven years on you!"

"My sister is right," said Ned suspiciously. "The duke was a friend of our grandfather's. You certainly were not his old school chum!"

"No, I had not that honor—though my father did," replied the duke. "You speak of my father—though he was not gouty and had every intention of coming up here to make your acquaintance. His illness prevented him—he died some nine months ago—and passed your care on to me."

The twins made no comment to this as they exchanged glances; however, the duke continued, "It would appear that I have done a poor job of it. However . . . no matter . . . I intend to settle this affair as quickly as possible."

Mandy was incensed by his attitude. He treated them like children caught in a bog of their own making, and she had no liking of such treatment.

"You needn't exert yourself on our account, Your Grace."

"Do not for a moment think that is what I am doing," he said honestly. "It is for my own interests that I apply myself. I owe my family name the respect it

deserves. As you have involved yourselves—and therefore my name—in scandal, it is my duty to see to it
that the grime is dispensed with."

"Oh! Why . . . that is beyond everything the most
selfish!" breathed Mandy with undisguised contempt.
"What a perfectly horrid . . . selfish man you are!"

The duke had never been told this before and, though
he knew it to be perfectly true, he was irked by the
insult. He was used to having maids of all sorts fawning
over him; however, he had no time to deliver a setdown, for Ned was calling his attention. "Look, Mandy,
Your Grace, I think we had better move away from the
road."

"My intentions exactly," said the duke. "Pick up
your pistol and my driver's and mount up. Your sister
and I shall follow on her horse."

"I shall not ride with you!" protested Mandy, "I will
ride with my brother."

"No, Miss Sherborne. I have no faith in the pair of
you. You might take it into your heads to vanish, and
I have no wish to search you out at this time of night—
though search you out I would. Now come. 'Tis time
you showed me where you have been hiding yourselves
these two weeks."

Ned hoisted himself into his saddle and watched with
some inward amusement as the duke pulled Mandy up
onto the horse, situating her not before him, but at his
back. She sat awkwardly clutching the leather of the
saddle rather than holding on to the duke, and suddenly
they were bounding forward at a canter. She slid about
uncomfortably, until the duke aware of her predicament, laughed and reached for her arms, "Hold me,
Miss Sherborne. I assure you, the proprieties you have

already flaunted far outweigh any that may be discarded by your holding on to me!"

This in no way mollified Miss Sherborne. However, the pace back to the Abbey was such that she had no choice in the matter. She sat stiffly, holding his waist and staring at his back, chagrined that he had chosen to seat her there rather than before him. Really, she thought irritably, he was the most ungallant man she had ever met.

As they approached the Abbey ruins, they slowed and she glanced about warily for any chance travelers. When they were fairly certain no one was about, they made for the ruins straight and quick. They dismounted and led the horses to the far building, where they lit a lantern after closing the door and bedded down their mounts for the night. The duke said little as this was done and Mandy removed the straw to expose the trap door. They made their way slowly down the steps, along the low narrow corridor of stone and earth to the dim, vaulted chamber at the end.

As they entered, Chauncy awoke with a snort and knuckled his eyes when they chanced across the duke's splendid form. "Coo . . . Lud bless ye, loveys! What 'ave ye brought me?"

Chapter Six

Viscount Skippendon's dark coach rolled easily over the surprisingly smooth main pike. It was a bright summer day, and the sun gave its rays lovingly, spreading warmth over the harebells. The purple tints of heather brushed the breeze with a gentle scent as the black carriage passed. Refreshed by a night's rest, the viscount's driver had put away all thoughts of highwaymen and the like and was whistling cheerfully, content to be part of the fine morning. However, his passenger noticed neither the sparkle of the day, nor the loveliness of the passing landscape. The Duke of Margate had not passed a good night, and he had been up and about too early to contemplate the poetic beauty of a summer's day!

The duke sat back in the coach, his hat on the seat before him as were his shining hessians. His blue eyes were veiled and his face drawn in deep thought. The events of the previous evening and again this morning had left him deeply disturbed. His meeting with Chauncy last night had gone from close-mouthed suspicion on the groom's part to sudden undisguised frankness. The duke had flung one direct question after another at both Ned and his groom and after a time found himself in possession of all the pertinent details of the Sherborne dilemma. This led him to three sure conclusions: he found he liked Lord Sherborne; he knew him to be innocent of the crime of which he was accused; and the young man's prospects looked grim indeed.

The duke had risen from the hour-long session in the damp underground cell the twins had fashioned for themselves deeply troubled by all he had learned. He had discovered from this interview that Chauncy's loyalty to the twins was not to be questioned, that Mandy's determination to shield her brother was as indomitable as her hoyden spirit, and that the object of all this attention was as fine a gentle young buck as ever he had encountered. However, these observations gave him no aid in discerning a way out of their entanglement. Thus it was he chose this morning to visit Squire Bevis and Alfred Speenham. He would know more of these particular relations—and of their intentions.

The squire's home was excellently maintained but of modest proportions. Its Tudor walls were acceptably mellowed and boasted a lush growth of ivy. The house and its simple holdings dated back some hundred years and provided its present master (who chanced to inherit the entirety when its late squire died without the benefit of direct issue) a comfortable if not luxurious means of independence.

As the viscount's coach with its single occupant approached the short straight drive, the duke sat up and perched his top hat rakishly over one eye (more from habit than concern). He surveyed his surroundings with calculated interest. It would appear, thought he, that Ned's uncle was not in need of funds . . . though, in truth, according to the Sherborne legacy entailment, Squire Bevis would stand to gain absolutely nothing by removal of its lord. The Sherborne estate and all its blunt would first go to Amanda.

The driver halted the coach and jumped down to open the door for His Grace, for he had already benefited from the duke's generosity and was well disposed to serve. The duke leaped nimbly down and adjusted his summer weight pale green superfine cutaway before going up the three stone steps to the dark oak door. He was met by a squat butler to whom he presented his card. Silently the butler perused the duke's card, then regarded the duke with the awe of one who finds himself for the first time in his life in the presense of royalty!

"You may advise the squire that I am here on a matter of utmost urgency and hope he will forgive my sudden appearance," said the duke pleasantly.

The butler looked stricken indeed. "I regret, Your Grace—most assuredly I do—that the squire is away from home."

"And Mr. Speenham—is he also away from home?"

The butler beamed, pleased to find a question he could respond to in the affirmative.

"Mr. Speenham is in the morning room taking breakfast."

"Then if you will be so kind as to take him my card, I shall be pleased to wait here," said the duke, dropping his gloves and top hat on the wall table beside him.

The butler made a slight bow and hurried off. When he returned, it was with a smile of one who has just found favor in his employer's eyes. The duke was led down a narrow dark hall to the rear of the house and found himself in a surprisingly bright but small room, facing a young man whom Beau Brummell would have shuddered to gaze upon. Gold dressing gown flowing, pomaded locks glistening, and hand extended, Alfred Speenham came forward enthusiastically, every bit as awed as his butler at discovering a noble duke gracing his halls.

"How can I express my . . . my infinite delight at your presence in my home?" greeted Mr. Speenham, giving His Grace a limp handshake. "Please . . . do come . . . sit . . . join me at my breakfast table. 'Tis but a simple one as I detest the sight of red meat in the morning, but I can have some brought up for you if you like."

"That is unnecessary, sir, I have already breakfasted," said the duke determined to be friendly but already finding this difficult. He took the chair Mr. Speenham indicated and sat facing his host. "No doubt, Mr. Speenham . . . you may have guessed why I am here."

Alfred Speenham managed a grave expression. "Ah, yes, these weeks have been simply dreadful, both for my father and myself. You can have no notion what it is like to have one's name connected with a murderer. Why, I have been avoiding all activity in hopes that the talk may subside."

"I sympathize with you," rejoined the duke, itching to give him a proper setdown but far too wise to yield to this inclination.

"My father has today gone to Teeside for he received word from a friend that my cousin Edward was seen in that vicinity," said Alfred, lowering his voice conspiratorily.

"Then you and your father both believe Lord Sherborne guilty of the crime in question?" asked the duke, playing idly with the spoon nearest his fingertips.

Alfred Speenham's eyes narrowed, and he appraised his guest silently for a moment. Certainly the fellow had a great deal of style and address. He was younger than he had supposed the twins' guardian to be . . . but was he merely a corinthian as his figure and deportment suggested? How astute was he? After all, it was to the duke's favor to have Edward Sherborne cleared and thereby secure the safety of his own name, surmised Alfred, not quite the fool he was often dubbed. His answer came slowly as though each word were carefully chosen.

"Ah . . . do *we* think him guilty? You know, of course, that he had been meeting poor Celia— clandestinely—and there is that page from her diary . . . and there is Aunt Agatha swearing that Celia was forcing his hand. Yes, I am afraid that Edward— spoiled, devil-may-care Edward—wanted out of the situation and never dreamed that Sir Owen would catch him very nearly in the act."

"And . . . his sister?"

"Amanda . . . my poor darling Amanda? Why she had nothing to do with that at all. No, no. However, she is his twin and inclined to impulsiveness. One must not really blame her for her misguided action in taking part later . . . to . . . rescue Edward. No, indeed. Precisely what m'father was saying this very morning before he left for Teeside. Said, 'mark me, Alfred. Amanda is a spirited female, but we'll not let her be ruined by herself. I'll find her; and she'll have to come to her senses,' " quoted Alfred with a sigh.

"Am I to understand that your father intends to locate his nephew and bring him in to stand trial? Then what of his niece?" The duke was unable to disguise his displeasure at this point.

"Oh, you needn't worry on that score. Papa is quite certain he can bring her through this, for you must know that we had plans to become engaged—before all this," said Alfred blandly.

"*You* and Miss Sherborne had plans?" asked the duke with some astonishment.

"Well, Amanda and I had never discussed it formally. But . . ."

"I see," interpolated the duke. "But to get back to the meat of the matter. We must remember that there is bound to be mud slung about, and as you and your father are related to the Sherbornes and I am also connected, some of that dirt is bound to come our way."

"Exactly so. But there seems to be nothing for it," sighed Alfred, not overly concerned.

The duke tried a new approach. "Were you well acquainted with poor Miss Brinley? Was she lovely—the poor thing?"

"Celia . . . was exquisite—in some ways much

more so than Amanda. Celia was sophisticated . . . womanly . . ." Alfred suddenly caught himself up short.

"Odd," said the duke to bait him.

"What is?"

"That Miss Brinley should have set her cap for young Sherborne when she had *you* in the vicinity," said the duke lightly.

His vanity was fluffed, and he rose to the occasion. "Exactly so, and she did not find me unattractive, but I imagine she was well aware that my father would never countenance the match. The fact is that he had no use for Celia. Thought her beneath my touch, and my father made it quite clear that I would be cut from his will should I consider any female not of his approval," Speenham confided.

"So . . . knowing this she cast her lures toward young Sherborne."

"Precisely so. Though, not until recently . . . always wondered whom she had cast her cap at before . . ." he said meditatively.

"Then you believe there was someone else . . . ?" asked the duke intently.

"No, no. Yet . . . there could have been. Some said she had a decided partiality for Viscount Skippendon, but in truth I never saw them together. Probably all a hum!"

"I see," said the duke quietly.

Mandy awoke with a start and gazed about her dark surroundings. She propped herself up on the straw bed and peered through the bleakness of her chamber and sensed rather than saw that she was alone. She lit the tallow in the pewter holder beside her straw and spotted there a piece of scribbled notepaper.

Mandy—
Don't fret. The duke came by with my horse and sent us off on a little errand. I'll explain later. He said *you* weren't to stir from the Abbey! So don't!

Ned

Mandy (as she often reminded her twin) had entered the world a good four minutes before him. She was his elder, his confidante, his faithful friend—but she was not in the habit of receiving orders from him. When those orders originated from the lips of one Brock Haydon, Duke of Margate, she found herself ready to explode with indignation. Ha! Stay at the Abbey . . . alone? With nothing but a book to keep me company? Ha! Thundered Miss Sherborne to her empty chamber and with considerable heat. The fact that, until she read her brother's laconic epistle, she had had every intention of resting in the shade of the Abbey's safe grounds with the newly published *Pride and Prejudice* by Jane Austen did little to mollify her injured ego.

She was feeling quite abused, for really had she not been literally left in the dark while Ned, Chauncy, and the odious duke schemed and plotted? Monstrous beings these . . . treating her as though she were some ordinary female . . . with nothing to do but sit about and wait as ordered. Well, not she! Mandy went with some violence to the tin bowl of washwater Chauncy had thoughtfully provided and proceeded to dissolve the night's grime. She donned a fresh white linen shirt, pleased that it had dried since yesterday's washing, and pulled on a pair of her brother's old buckskin breeches. With the benefit of a small hand mirror she brushed out her hair and tied it at the top of her head so that its long curls dropped in provocative profusion about her face. Her bullycock hat was scooped up, the candle smothered, and out she went.

The sun and fresh air was so refreshing that Mandy nearly forgot her turbulence. The breeze pressed her open-necked shirt against her body and delivered the scent of lavender and heather to her senses, carrying her back to another time. She remembered when she and Ned played amongst the stones of the Abbey ruins as children. They had gone into sectioned rooms where the sky lay open above them and weeds had replaced the flooring. Mandy used to pretend she could still hear the echo of the monks' steps over the limestone footing as they made their way to chapel. Nothing was left of the vaulted ceilings and stained glass; there were only crumbling walls and pillars and bits of stone foundations. She had loved it here as a child; she loved it still. But she was in a strange mood and not content to dream of history. She needed to walk. She was restless—and she needed to work off her evil temper. But where would it be safe?

She left her hat perched on a mound of weeds and stared across the vastness of the purple glen before her. The dark, looming forest seemed almost to curl a tantalizing finger, making the decision for her. A silver rill trickled through the woods . . . and she had a sudden longing to dip her toes into its cool ripples. With an impulsive decision she ran through the full blooms of heather, dashing wildly for the safety of the dark forest, and stumbling over an old fallen oak when she at last arrived.

She had to make out her own path, trampling down low bushes and picking her way through the tangle until she found a narrow passage through the maze of trees and brush. This led to the freshwater stream she remembered, and she dropped down its bank onto the pebbles and removed her boots and stockings. She splashed her feet in the cold water and after a time felt some peace restored. She sighed, for though the duke was a provoking creature, he had been correct in telling her to remain at the Abbey. 'Twas safest. But, she thought, he was such an arrogant, selfish, conceited, horrid . . . Oh! It tickled her subconscious that he was also quite undeniably handsome. However, this thought was immediately put aside. Handsome . . . bah! It didn't signify. He was loathsome.

What was even more annoying was the fact that both Ned and Chauncy seemed to have been won over by him. When the duke had left them last evening— taking Chauncy's horse in his offhand way, saying he would return it himself in the morning—she had turned to her brother to declare that never before had she seen a man so puffed up in his own consequence and that she had no great liking for their guardian.

"Really?" answered Ned with some surprise. "He seems rather a nice chap—a bit stiff—but a right 'un all the same."

"How can you say so?" snapped Mandy. "He . . . he thinks himself a demigod . . . capable of all things."

"That he does," agreed Chauncy, momentarily gratifying her but adding, "that he does, missy. But make no mistake, could be 'cuz he be well able to 'andle most things!"

"Oh!" screeched Mandy, much overset. "He has you both befuddled!"

Chauncy grinned but said nothing to this as he bade them good-night and made his way to the room above the tunnel.

Her thoughts carried her for a time until she brought herself up short. She had gone too far, she was being foolish, she might be seen—for the path was widening as was the stream. Quickly she turned back, but before she had taken a step a male voice halted her.

"Amanda!"

She closed her eyes, but there was nothing for it but to turn and meet her fate head on. If she were to run now, she would only lead him to Ned.

"Sir Owen . . . how are you?" asked Mandy as nonchalantly as though she were meeting him in a drawing room.

He stood some twenty feet before her, a fishing rod in his hand, his rugged face enigmatic. She noted that he looked thinner than usual—but perhaps it was because he wore only his shirtsleeves and buckskin waistcoat. His topboots were muddied, and the basket containing the fish he'd caught was at his feet. He dropped the rod and came forward, and she saw the look of concern in his hazel eyes.

"How am I? My God!" he said as he reached her and suddenly scooped her into his embrace. She put her hand to his chest to maintain a respectable distance.

"Sir Owen, release me do . . . or is it your intention to turn me over to the authorities as you did my brother?"

He tightened his hold, and his expression was grim, "Is that what you think? Amanda, how did you get such a notion? It wasn't what I told your uncle that sent him hotfoot after your brother. Egad! How would it serve my purpose to be the cause of your brother's entrapment?"

"What purpose?" asked Mandy frowning, temporarily forgetting that she was locked in his arms.

"To make you my wife," he said, moving his head downwards. She put up her hand and covered his mouth. "Release me, Sir Owen," she said without fear.

"Promise me," he said raising his head, "that you will not scurry away."

"You are being outrageous!"

"Promise me."

"Never! You behave . . . a scoundrel."

"Amanda, listen to me. I have been searching out this Elly Bonner . . . trying to get hold of the diary, for I am certain therein lies the key."

"Oh . . . oh, Sir Owen . . . if you could only do that . . ." cried Mandy hopefully. 'We haven't had any luck at all."

"And if I could free Ned . . . would you be mine?" he asked quietly.

"But . . . but I don't love you," said Mandy, dismayed.

"That doesn't matter. You would in time. Answer me Mandy, is that your price?"

"I . . . I don't know. Please . . . don't press me . . . I . . . I have to think."

Sir Owen's hazel eyes narrowed as he remembered

Viscount Skippendon. Here, he thought, was his rival. Had she not always spoken of Skippy with enthusiasm? Was it not to the viscount that she went running the morning after Celia's murder? And the viscount—was there not something odd about *his* movements?

"Amanda, there is something I must tell you, because there is someone you trust implicitly that perhaps you should not."

"What do you mean? Oh, do release me, Sir Owen," said Mandy, struggling again.

He chuckled, took her hand, and pulled her down to a fallen log. "Very well . . . if you will sit beside me."

"It seems I have little choice. But do explain. Whom should I not trust?"

" 'Tis the viscount, Amanda," he said gravely.

"Skippy? You must be jesting?" disbelief in her voice.

"Unfortunately, I am not. My valet has a friendship of sorts with the viscount's gentleman and, while I ordinarily discourage gossip being carried from one servant to the other, I believed in this case it was necessary to make an exception. You see, I have been informed that the viscount was for some time carrying on an intimate relationship with Miss Brinley—and one that he wished terminated because he had picked up with yet another female."

"Stop it! I don't believe a word of this. You cannot really mean that you think Skippy capable of . . . murder?"

"Only that I know Ned did not murder your cousin." He slipped his arm round her slim waist and brought her hand to his lips, "I want to protect you . . . protect Ned. Let me."

Chapter Seven

The duke left the squire's estates behind
him, but he brought a troubled countenance to the
viscount's manor. Skip was not at home and none of
his servants were able to tell the duke whither their
master had gone. The duke had his stallion saddled
and proceeded to take the short-cut he had discovered
that morning to the Abbey ruins. His horse was
closeted and Mandy's discarded bullycock hat found
before he set out in search of his missing ward. It was
not difficult to decide that she had made for the
woods—her horse was stabled—where else would she
go? He took the shortest path across the glen, correctly assuming that she would walk away from the
road not toward it. Once at the edge of the trees it
was easy to see where the lady had made her path. He

discovered her direction in time to catch Sir Owen's impassioned expression as he took Mandy into his arms and lovingly kissed her hand.

As her guardian the Duke was entitled to feel a bit of prudish annoyance; however, he experienced a disproportionate degree of irritation in keeping with this status. Clearly a decision must now be made— whether to go forward and confront the lovers, putting an end to their romantic interlude, or to remain watching and await the outcome. Both of these fancies were so unlike his image of himself that he quickly rejected both these notions with some violence. He turned his back on the pair and made his way back to the Abbey to await his ward's return.

Mandy was finally able to persuade Sir Owen to take his leave of her. She watched him ride away, waiting until he had rounded the bend in the road before scurrying through the woods, sure that he had no time to retrace his path to pursue her. Sir Owen felt confident that she trusted him and he had no wish to endanger that trust. Hence he made no attempt to follow—her direction he could find later!

Breathless, her shirt askew and her curls tumbling down her back in wild but tantalizing disarray, Mandy rushed the Abbey center. She leaned against a stone wall to catch her breath when she suddenly lost it once again. Standing directly before her, his broad shoulder resting against a corner wall, his black silky waves blowing about his handsome head, stood the Duke of Margate . . and there was something in his blue eyes that made Mandy tremble.

He quizzed her with his direct gaze, bringing the

blush to her already heightened color and making her
feel like a silly child. Slowly, disapprovingly, his glance
swept her disheveled condition.

"Well, well, my rough-and-tumble ward . . .
where have you been?"

" 'Tis not for you to question my activities," said
the lady with as much pluck as she could muster.

"Indeed . . . is it not? I regret to inform you, my
dear child, that you are much mistaken in such notions.
You and your twin have made your activites very
much my affair!" replied the duke sardonically.

"As to that, we did not ask you to come here—and
we did not ask for your help, Your Grace—or should
I address you as Uncle Brock? Really . . . how does
one address one's guardian?" demanded the lady with
considerable spirit.

The idea of having himself addressed as Uncle
Brock by a grown female, who under ordinary circumstances might have enjoyed the duke's gallantry, so
disturbed him that he lost his sense of composure. He
drew himself up to his full six feet and glared.

"Certainly not! I have the good fortune *not* to claim
blood ties between us . . . and prefer to keep it that
way! However, I *am* your guardian, my dear, and will
be so for some months yet. I will know *here and now*
what the deuce you mean by going about the countryside dressed so improperly!"

She glanced down at herself and noted that her
shirt had come open exposing a great deal more than
was modestly allowable. She bit her lip and held her
shirt closed over her bosom.

"I . . . I went for . . . a walk."

"May I remind you that you are in hiding—due to your own folly—and that such walks could endanger your brother's safety!" snapped the duke.

"I was very careful that no one should see me," said she defensively.

His brow went up. "You are certain no one saw you?"

She found herself avoiding his eye and in spite of her defiance, a guilty wave stole through her.

"No one followed me here."

"Ah . . . you think to play a game of semantics with me, child. No one followed you here. But what of the friendly fellow in the woods? Does he know about your hideaway? Or is he just someone to pass the tedium of the day with?"

Faith, she thought, he had seen her with Sir Owen! Oh! What he must think? Then after a moment's confusion: How dare he spy on her? How dare he think she was carrying on with Sir Owen?

"The manner in which I spend my time is my own affair!" countered the lady, her face red with fury.

"Do you think so indeed? May I remind you that you will not leave the circumference of my protection—and therefore my family name—for some time yet. Therefore you will behave in a manner I deem fit."

Mandy could not believe his gall or the mortification he was able to drag her through. She stamped her foot and shouted, "Go to the devil! And may the demons seize your notions of propriety!" Whereupon she spun on her heel and would have bolted had he not reached out and clamped his hand round her slender arm.

"Take heed, m'girl! You are not speaking to your groom or your brother, and I am well able to administer the spanking you obviously stand in need of!" His eyes sparkled dangerously.

"You wouldn't dare!" she hissed. For a split second the duke nearly forgot that she was his ward. He saw before him a spitfire, and he burned with a sudden urge to kiss her. Instead, he spoke, his voice controlled and hard.

"You think not?"

She didn't doubt for a moment that he would, and lest he try, she restrained a retort but yanked her arm out of his grip, hurting herself in the process. She winced at the pain. Noting this he would have moved forward to see if he had injured her when the sound of horses brought him to a sharp alert.

"Get into the stable!" he ordered in low, hurried tones.

She complied without demur, but a few moments later the sound of her brother's voice brought her out once again. "Ned," she cried, coming out, "you horrid thing, what do you mean going off without me?"

He grinned as he dismounted and gave his reins to Chauncy.

"Couldn't very well take you. Must see that girl," offered her brother. "Hullo, Duke."

"I don't see that at all, you wretch! Why could you not?"

"Duke here pointed it out. Said we would be seen for twins. Might catch a curious eye in Wharfedale."

"Oh," said she in a small voice. "Well . . . why did you go there?"

"I sent them!" said the duke curtly, transferring his gaze from her incredulous expression to that of Lord Sherborne's lively countenance.

"You . . . you sent them?" seethed Mandy. "How could you? Faith, they could have been recognized! Why, of all the addle-brained things to have done . . ."

The duke held his temper and said in a low, dangerous tone that cut short her abuse, "I think you have said enough! Perhaps you have no interest in finding Elly Bonner . . . *I do*. As it happens I am not acquainted with the elusive girl—your brother and groom are. I relied on Chauncy's instincts to keep them both from curious eyes . . . and apparently my faith was not misplaced!"

"You still sent them into danger."

"Go and take a damper, Mandy," grinned her brother. "Whatever ails you?"

"Well, I just don't like it—none of it. It seems very odd to me that the duke should send you into danger. I mean really—what could he have learned since he left us last night to make him think Elly Bonner was in Wharfedale?"

The duke gave her his back and said to Ned with a sigh, "Sherborne, if you will . . . I fear I have not the patience to explain myself to a gamine of a girl!"

Ned grinned appreciatively. "Lord, Mandy, ole girl, no need to get yourself hipped over it. The duke here had it last night from Aunt Agatha's maid that Elly might be in or near Wharfedale."

"Oh . . ." managed Mandy. "But still . . . it all seems a bit . . ."

"Lookee 'ere, missy . . . stop yer prattle o'er this fetch. I dessay the duke 'ere 'ad enuff things cluttering his 'ead," offered Chauncy, cutting her off. Chauncy bit hard on a piece of dried beef as though for emphasis. He then sought out a high clump of overgrown weeds and grass and dropped onto its mound with a weary sigh. "As it 'appens, missy, we owe the duke a measure of gratitude, coz if we 'adn't piked over to Wharfedale, we wouldn't a learnt about Hawkins!"

The duke's straight black brows curved upwards inquiringly, and his blue eyes seemed to penetrate Chauncy's mind as he said in a low voice and with narrowed interest, "Hawkins?"

"Ay, and a thousand pities we couldn't a stayed a mite longer and prigged this 'ere Hawkins' direction, Yer Grace. But had this need to shake our shambles out of the Red Hart Inn . . . reel suddenlike."

"Oh? Something make you fidgety?" inquired the duke.

Ned slapped Chauncy's shoulder before dropping down beside him on the clump of earth.

"Lord, no, duke! Don't let Chauncy bamboozle you . . . he enjoyed every minute of it. Certes, Mandy, wait till you hear!"

"Hear . . . hear what?" cried Mandy with some exasperation.

"We hobnobbed with a redbreast," declared Ned giving them a settler and grinning all the while. "A Bow Street runner—a London runner!" He said this as though he were telling a hilarious jest.

Mandy was not amused. "What?" she shrieked.

"Famous good sport!" added her brother, lest she think he had not enjoyed the encounter.

"Oh, Ned, no," said Mandy, dismayed. "Never say so. But how . . . why?"

"I should like to return to the beginning—if we may," interpolated the duke authoritatively, "if you will kindly inform us who Hawkins may be and what he has to do with Elly Bonner?"

"But they were stopped by a runner!" snapped Mandy rounding on him angrily.

"No, I believe they managed to have a conversation with the illustrious fellow, and I am quite certain we shall hear all about it. However, for the time being we shall forego that particular treat and return to the issue at hand—Hawkins, if you please."

"Oh—Hawkins," said Ned coming down a peg and thinking the duke was turning them up dull for no purpose. "Don't know what good that piece of business will be to us."

"Nevertheless, young man," said the duke, making Ned feel every bit a school boy, "you will do me the honor of imparting your information to me and then allowing me to decide as to its value."

Ned blushed and his sister took umbrage on his behalf, casting the duke a scathing glance. However, it was at this particular juncture that she happened to note that the duke's glossy hair waving in the breeze was nearly blue in the intensity of its blackness, and that his profile was ruggedly handsome. As though the duke sensed her scrutiny, he glanced her way, and her expression gave rise to a twinkle in his blue eyes. She caught the glance and put up her chin, looking away haughtily.

"Well, Chauncy has this friend at the Red Hart. And though he doesn't know Elly, he knows this Hawkins, though he doesn't know where Hawkins is . . ." began Ned rather vaguely.

The duke put up his hands in an explicit show of impatience, before turning to Chauncy.

"Perhaps, Chauncy, you may be able to tell me *who the devil Hawkins is*?"

"Aye, that I can and be glad to do it," said Chauncy, brushing his hands together for he had finished his beef and was well disposed now to conversation. "He be Elly Bonner's man!"

"Ned! Chauncy! Why, that is beyond everything great!" cried Mandy, lighting up considerably.

The duke watched her thoughtfully for a moment before commenting.

"I see . . . and . . .?"

"That's it, Duke," said Ned ruefully. "Said 'twas a bit of useless news."

"Perhaps not, Ned. Did you get Hawkins' description . . . his habits . . . haunts?"

" 'ave it he be a big cove, Yer Grace—a sight larger than me—squareset, thick-jawed, and mean! A vulgar make-bait by all accounts and, wot's more, 'tis said he don't pound deal!"

Ned leaned over to where his sister had curled up and whispered in a low voice.

"Eh, Mandy, that's a piece of cant I ain't heard. What's pound-dealing?"

She smiled and answered in a similar whisper, "Honest work, Neddy."

"Thought so," said Ned before returning to the conversation that had continued in spite of their whispers.

". . . 'tis said too, Yer Grace, that Hawkins rode the high toby a bit," Chauncy said thoughtfully.

"But what else? Surely if you got that much, you must have learned his whereabouts." said the duke.

Chauncy shook his head sadly. "Hawkins ain't been seen these three weeks and more."

"And what of Elly . . . were you able to learn anything about her?" asked Mandy hopefully.

"More's the pity, missy . . . not a word on Elly Bonner," Chauncy replied, still shaking his head. "Funny thing, too . . . m'friend heard tell how Elly be a prime mort . . . not up to the bobbery of 'er covey! But there now! No telling wot fetch a mort will take into her noddle when her 'eart be in it!" pronounced Chauncy with a sigh.

"Then it is as Ned says. You were exposed to considerable danger and risks . . . all for nought!" said Mandy, casting an accusing eye towards the duke.

"Hold a moment, girl," exclaimed her twin. "Never said anything of the sort—at least not like that."

"But you said yourself that you were stopped by a Bow Street runner," said Mandy with some annoyance.

"Yes, indeed," agreed the duke, his eyes twinkling, "I do seem to recall your saying something about a redbreast?"

"By Jove, yes," said Ned cheering up. "We noted this stranger come into the inn, and he had a look about him. Didn't note it myself, but Chauncy did. Chauncy said he looked neither cit, farmer, nor gentleman, and rather thought 'twas time we loped off. We was on our way out when the fellow up and raises his bumper of ale and calls on the weather for conversation. We nodded that, yes, 'twas fit for human endurance, when he would have us join him in a drink. We tried to cry off, but he would hear nothing of it. Tipped his duff hat and says his name is Fowler and that he is looking to lease summer lodges! Summer lodges . . . if that don't look smoky . . . but I still didn't know what his lay was. Chauncy did, of course, but he couldn't get it across to me."

"How did you know he was a runner?" put in Mandy, wide-eyed.

"He gave me pricklies down me spine, he did. Suspicioned he was a redbreast the moment I clapped eyes on him. You see, he was tallow-faced and had cat-sticks for legs . . . laid all doubt to rest when he give us his name . . ."

"Oh, my God!" cried Mandy, putting a hand to her mouth. "That's right! He's the one staying in Harrowgate. Neddy, he must have your description and Chauncy's . . . that's why he stopped you . . ."

"Now, missy, don't take on so. As it happens I don't think he was interested in us . . . no . . . seemed to be more interested in the lay of land."

"Of course he was," exclaimed Mandy. "If he *is* looking for Neddy, he would want to know where he might be hiding."

"Did he inquire after the Abbey?" asked the duke quietly, a frown shading his eyes.

"No . . . wanted to know about the York Road . . . whether there were any old quarries off the route. Asked whether there were any hidden caves of limestone like the one up at the Peak . . . said he was interested in such things," said Ned.

"Aye. Told him we wasn't familiar with the area, being strangers 'ere ourselves. But this noddle 'ere . . . " he said, indicating Ned, "had a mind to be helpful and started to describe a track of canyon off the

Wharfe River and would have gone on if I hadn't near thought to spill his ale!"

"Well . . . I didn't know he was a runner then . . . did I?" defended Ned indignantly.

"Should 'ave . . . told ye there was a man callin' 'imself Fowler stayin' up at the Cock Pit . . . told ye least night he might be a runner!" said Chauncy unmercifully.

Ned eyed him a moment as though preparing a retaliation when Chauncy produced another length of dried beef and tossed it into his lap. Ned's glance shifted and, though it wasn't to his particular taste, hunger won out. Under Chauncy's twinkling eye and the duke's amused countenance, Ned began to chew.

Mandy gaped at them a moment and remembered that she was hungry. She watched her brother eat and was about to bring down a diatribe of abuse on his head when a loaf of bread dropped into her lap. She looked up to see Chauncy hand the duke a bottle of wine and the duke reward the groom with a wide smile. It struck her odd that the duke had a surprisingly boyish grin at times.

Further delectables were produced from Chauncy's saddlebags, and the company fell upon the cheese and apples with eager relish. When Mandy was at last satisfied, she sat back and sighed, frowned, and summed up. "So . . . what we now know is that Elly must be somewhere with a fellow who would as soon stab us as speak to us—and that a Bow Street runner is here looking for our place of sanctuary."

"Appearances are often deceiving, Amanda. We mustn't jump to the wrong conclusions simply for lack of better ones," said the duke, more to himself than to her.

"I haven't given you leave to use my first name, Your Grace, and I don't see that I am jumping to conclusions!" snapped Mandy.

"You needn't give me leave, child. I am your guardian, much as we both wish otherwise!" retorted the duke, his blue eyes flashing hard, "As to the runner . . . we shall have to use caution. It may be he is *not* searching Ned out."

"Then what is he doing here?" demanded she.

"At the moment, I haven't the slightest notion—indeed, we have only our suspicions to put him as a runner. He may in fact be something else altogether!"

Chapter Eight

Brock Haydon, eighth Duke of Margate, entered Viscount Skippendon's well-ordered home just as the sun had settled in the west. It was apparent to all he encountered that it was not one of his finer days. Sticwell, as excellent a butler as any could want, did his best to dispel some of His Grace's black mood by inquiring after his needs. There were but two, one being the viscount, (who, he was advised, was closeted with his man of business) and the other, a decanter of brandy. Sticwell immediately led him to the library where the garden doors had been thrown open to allow the cool breeze full access. The brandy was presented, and a footman sent off to the viscount.

Having dismissed the obsequious butler, the duke

ambled over to the glass door and leaned hard against
its frame. One hand troubled his hair while his eyes
concentrated on the red roses before him. He then
brought up the glass of brandy and shifted his gaze to its
dark inviting hue before swiftly and suddenly downing
the entire contents. A sort of fiend was working at his
brain, agonizingly demanding answers—and he had not
one to put on the table. The Sherborne twins—Lord
help me! he thought wretchedly. For here was the essence of all his woes. Hell and brimstone! Was there
ever such a scrape? Blister it! And he poured himself
another glass.

He moved to the yellow brocade sofa and sank into its
cushioned depths with a muffled thud. The situation
confronting him was a great deal more than just another challenge; and what was worse, the motive that
had brought him willy-nilly to Yorkshire seemed rather
obscure and insignificant. Scandal—that was it, wasn't
it? Well, if that had been his first consideration, it no
longer was. What did he care for such frippery now? He
only knew he wanted his wards returned to the safety
and comfort of their home—why didn't matter. Indeed,
he did not take the time to consider this very interesting
question. He knew himself won over somehow, captivated for no real reason. To be sure, the lad—Ned—
was certainly a charming scamp. And Amanda—'twas
true he longed, itched in fact, to give her a spanking—
yet he rather admired her spirit and her pluck. Very
well then, he was committed to them.

Sticwell, brushing at a speck of dust on his dark
coat, hurried forward clucking his tongue and wondering who it was now at the front door. He opened wide

the great oak door to allow an unfamiliar but certainly fashionable gentleman to stride languidly into the central hall. He then received the gentleman's buff-colored top hat and kid gloves.

"Thank you, good fellow. Be so kind as to advise the viscount that Sir Owen Turndale would like but a few moments with him."

The butler bowed politely. "Very good, sir. The viscount, however, is at the moment occupied. You may wish to wait in the library and join His Grace in a glass of brandy."

"His Grace?" asked Sir Owen, putting up a brow.

"The Duke of Margate, sir," explained the butler, pleased to puff off the title and thus his employer's consequence.

"Thank you, indeed I shall," said Sir Owen, following Sticwell across the polished floor.

The open-necked shirt and buckskins Sir Owen had worn earlier that morning had been replaced with a modish short-tailed coat of bottle green and a buff-colored silk waistcoat. His hessians shown to perfection, and his neckcloth, though not as intricate as the fashionable waterfall, was most certainly done in good taste. His auburn hair now pomaded with Russian oil was set carefully au chérubin about his face. Thusly, he presented himself to the duke who sat brooding over his problems in the library.

His Grace sat up with some interest upon the newcomer's entrance, and a moment's scrutiny was enough to confirm his suspicions. If this was not the man he had seen with Mandy earlier that day, it was certainly his double. Sir Owen's brown eyes appraised the duke quickly as he smiled and stretched out his hand. The duke rose and accepted it, hearing Sticwell's announcement in the background. Sir Owen Turndale, though personally unknown to him, was a name he had heard mentioned by many of his cronies. Each had heard of the other, for they both enjoyed many of the same diversions; yet until today their hedonistic paths had never crossed. Much of this had to do with the duke's pride in his heritage and the limits he had set upon himself because of it.

As Sir Owen spoke, he wondered what the deuce had brought a man of the duke's stamp to Yorkshire.

"Well, well, Margate! Fancy that! Of all places to be bumping into you . . . Yorkshire!"

"Indeed, is it not odd? Our meeting was inevitable though, you know," said the duke, smiling.

"Inevitable?" rejoined Sir Owen archly.

"Why, yes, old man. We do travel in similar sets . . . and until you left London some time back, we had the same fireband taking our fancy. You departed, leaving the pretty lady to my care," said the duke with a devilish grin.

"No doubt you took excellent care of her?" rallied Sir Owen amicably.

"No, no doubt at all," answered the duke.

"What then tore you away and, of all places, to the wilds of Yorkshire?"

"The purple blooms of heather," answered the duke roguishly.

"Of course—how stupid of me not to have realized. It was not that which lured me though."

"Oh?" said the duke with more interest than he allowed himself to exhibit.

"It's no secret, Margate. Done-up . . . dished!"

"Sorry to hear it, old boy. But ruralizing won't solve that particular problem. They are bound to catch up with you," said the duke, resuming his seat and inviting Sir Owen to take another.

The latter smiled ruefully as he sat down upon a yellow brocaded Chippendale. "As to that . . . settled most of my debts, mortgaged my estates. Didn't like to do it, but there was nothing for it. Returning to London just now would be something I can ill afford—though I have a horse running—and who knows? In the meantime, I find some of the . . . beauty in Yorkshire enough to while away the time."

"Oh?" The duke's bright blue eyes grew suddenly hard as an inexplicable irritation jibed within his breast.

"Sir Owen," said the viscount, entering the room, hand outstretched in welcome. "This is an unexpected pleasure." He turned to the duke, "So sorry, Brock, to have kept you waiting. My dratted man wouldn't let me go. But I see you two have been amusing yourselves." At which point he poured himself a glass of brandy and joined them by pulling up a windsor chair and straddling it.

"What have you been up to, Sir Owen? I haven't seen you at the Cock Pit in a while. Come to think on it, not since my red took Wally's gray. Eh, that was a prime turn up, was it not?"

"Indeed it was, and I won a sizeable bundle on your red, but 'tis not about cocks I came, Skip," said Sir Owen, his face taking on a grave expression.

"Eh, whatever do you mean, Owen?" asked the viscount.

Sir Owen smiled apologetically at the duke. "I don't want to appear rude, but the matter that has brought me here concerns a mutual friend of ours, and I should like a word in private with Skippendon."

"Of course," said the duke, getting to his feet.

"Nonsense!" snapped the viscount. "If you are referring to young Sherborne, you may as well know here and now that the Duke of Margate is guardian to the twins. In fact it is their predicament that has brought him to Yorkshire!"

Sir Owen's jaw dropped slightly before he recovered himself. "I see . . . though I can not imagine how it came about."

The duke grinned good-naturedly. "Nor I, but it is the sorry truth."

"Very well then, gentlemen, I shall get to the point. Today, and quite by accident, I ran into Mand . . . Miss Sherborne . . . in the Abbey woods!"

"Good God! Whatever is the child running about for? But then, she was ever a madcap! Bound to land herself in the basket that way!"

"Exactly so! After all, there is no telling whom she may run into next—sporting about on the loose as she is. Try as I might, I was not successful in my attempts to persuade her to leave her jaunting about. She is determined to remain with her brother until he is cleared of the charges hanging over his head."

"Remain with her brother? Then you know where they have hidden themselves?" asked the duke slowly.

"No, she would not disclose that to me, and I did not want to betray her trust by following her. I believe that she and Ned and that groom of theirs must be staying in some hovel in the area . . . and, frankly, the thought of Mandy . . . Miss Sherborne . . . in such a situation is most distressing!"

"Indeed yes," said Skippendon, turning to the duke, "but it would appear that there is little we can do at the moment."

Sir Owen's brow went up. "That is very disheartening . . . and from one who calls himself their closest friend."

His hackles up, the viscount blushed. "Just what does being a friend require of me, Sir Owen? My time— they have it should they call for it, but they have not. My opinions—they are free whenever they wish them."

"I should think your action—without their asking!" snapped Sir Owen, frowning.

"Action? But what sort?" asked the viscount.

"Those charges are utterly ridiculous. We should be working to get them dismissed," returned Sir Owen.

"Just so. But how do you propose to accomplish such a feat?" retorted the viscount.

"What of the maid—this Elly Bonner? What have you done to find her?"

"I . . . I . . . have set about inquiries, of course. They turned up absolutely nothing. The girl has apparently vanished without a trace."

"And the diary?"

"In all probability it has been thrown into the fire," answered the viscount with a sigh.

"Well, I must say your attitude leaves much to be desired," concluded Sir Owen sardonically.

The duke had said nothing during this exchange, merely sitting back and watching the gentlemen do polite battle. Now, however, he interjected quietly and on his floundering friend's behalf.

"Just exactly what do you expect of the viscount, Sir Owen? For though you hurl questions at him in a tone I find most curious, you offer no answers."

"Answers? I don't really know that I have any . . . though I do have bits of a puzzle. I know, for example, that Elly Bonner was seen ten nights ago in York."

"Good God, man! How . . . ?" started the viscount.

The duke rose. "In York? Alone?"

"No, she was with some brute of a fellow. I had it from one of my servants."

"Did he see her himself?" continued the duke, acutely aware of his agitated heartbeat.

"No, he asked after her, and one of his friends mentioned seeing her. But I doubt that she is still there, for I sent a man immediately, and he could find no trace of her," answered Sir Owen with a sigh.

"Humph!" said the viscount.

"Eh, Skip . . . don't you believe it?" inquired the duke, one of his mobile brows uplifted.

"No, I do not! Think it is all a hum. Depend upon it, the poor wretched girl is dead."

"Upon my soul! What the deuce makes you think so?" ejaculated Sir Owen.

"Stands to reason, don't it? Look here—Ned was delayed from meeting Celia on time that evening because Elly took him a note—written, we must presume, by the murderer. Therefore, this Elly, not only had the information the diary contained—she also knew the murderer! *She had to be eliminated!*"

The duke folded his arms, bringing one hand up to his pursed mouth, and his blue eyes were dark with thought. "There is that. But you know, Skip, I am inclined to think the girl got away. Bolted, you know, the moment she heard Miss Celia was murdered."

"That would mean the murderer wants her as much as we do. 'Tis all the more reason for tearing the countryside apart until she is found," said Sir Owen rising to his feet, "and there is something else Skip—something that has been plaguing my mind . . ."

"Out with it, man! If you have something to ask, then ask. Don't stand about looking like a damnable judge!" said Skippendon, feeling as though he were being attacked.

"It's of a delicate nature—but very well—it has come to my attention that you and Celia were . . . intimately acquainted for some time," began Sir Owen cautiously.

"Good Lord! Is that all? As a matter of fact, and though 'tis none of your business, yes, we were close during the winter. It was over by spring. I don't mean to be glib about it, but there it is in a nutshell!" answered the viscount.

"No, not quite—for I believe that you are now seeing a young woman and that you have no wish for your connection to Miss Celia to be brought up."

The viscount took a step forward. "What are you intimating? Out with it, man! Do you think I murdered Celia rather than have my affair with her made known? Or are you thinking 'twas my babe she carried?"

It was at this moment that the duke stepped between the men, for clearly the viscount was in a fury and showed every sign of working it off physically. "Easy, Skip . . . you've become hot in hand since you've been in the country."

The viscount turned pale blue eyes upon his friend and there was a tremor in his voice. "Don't you realize what this blackguard is saying? Devil seize his heart and feed it to the lions! He has come into my home and hinted that not only am I a murderer but one who allows his friend to be hunted in his stead! I am going to land him a facer, here and now, Brock, so stand aside!"

The duke stood his ground. "You damn well won't! Is there not enough scandal without dragging your name—and perhaps that of the young lady you are now interested in—into this mess. Mark me, Skip— that is precisely what will happen if you two come to a mill in your home!"

The viscount stopped dead in his tracks and seeing this, the duke attempted to rally his usual good humor.

"There now, Skip—glad you saw the light, for in truth you've never been an out and outer—not handy with your fives, and Owen here looks as though he has sparred with the Gentleman himself!"

"I don't give a farthing for that!" snapped the viscount, not at all pleased with the sally.

"I'm quite certain you do not," grinned the duke before turning to Sir Owen. "You sir, have made your unwise and most rude conjecture and availed yourself of nought! I suggest you make your apology—if you are man enough—and take your leave!"

"Apology? Indeed, I see no reason for one. I have asked what needed to be asked and have not been satisfactorily answered. It was what any friend of the Sherbornes would have done. I have no recourse but to investigate all my suspicions. And Margate, rest assured that I shall!"

"Why does that sound like a threat? Or am I too under suspicion?" asked the duke, his blue eyes hard as ice.

"No threat is intended for the innocent. Good-day, gentlemen." Sir Owen turned on his heel, leaving Margate and the viscount to stare quietly at each other.

Chapter Nine

Mandy sat up and pushed the thin blanket away. The darkness of her self-imposed cell was all-encompassing, yet she strained through the blackness in an attempt to see her brother lying some few feet away. It was in vain, for though she could hear his light breathing, she could not make out his form. She tried calling to see if he were awake, "Ned . . . Neddy . . .?"

She received in response to this a severe grumble and thus gave up the effort with a weary sigh. It was musky and uncomfortable, and her straw bed was certainly not what she was used to; nor did time seem to be an aid to adjustment. Her small bones ached; she was dismal, restless; and her thoughts for no reason at all suddenly went to the duke. A fleeting sense of irritation permeated her spirit as his features appeared vividly to her mind. She gave her straw pillow a solid pounding and lay back with a thump. He was horrid . . . arrogant . . . a libertine . . . a rakehell. Here he was, lording it over them, treating her as a child. Well, she would certainly teach him a thing or two!

Indeed, thought Mandy militantly, what she needed was a plan of action. That was it, of course—action. She had to find Elly . . . and without the duke's odious help. But this was something Mandy knew she could not do alone. Chauncy and Ned, with their heads in danger, could be of little more assistance. So there was nothing for it but to turn to Sir Owen. It was not a decision she liked, for she was not sure she should trust him. He was most assuredly willing and capable. Yet there was something within him she could not like. Oh, pooh! She was being ridiculous. She closed her eyes, determined to sleep and put the duke out of her head. But this decision did little for her peace of mind. She lay awake in the darkness, still very restless, still feeling helpless, while the duke's eyes taunted her.

The Duke of Margate had not enjoyed his dinner with the viscount. He had found it both strange and trying. Skippy was unusually quiet and conspicuously dull. His habitual urbane manner had been shattered by a harsh black mood; his conversation was clipped almost to the point of rudeness.

"Skip, I have no wish to intrude on your privacy. But perhaps I may be able to help," offered the duke quietly as they sipped their port in the library afterwards.

"Help? Who said anything about needing help?" retorted the viscount, flushing slightly.

"No one did . . . nor did anyone have to," answered the duke, with some slight annoyance in his tone.

"Well don't need any. What's more . . . going to bed!" said the viscount suddenly.

"No, really, old boy. Doing too brown, ain't you? Going to bed at eight o'clock? What sort of gudgeon do you take me for?"

The viscount stopped and leveled his eyes on the duke's inquiring face.

"Devil is in it that . . . never mind . . . got this headache, Brock . . . don't feel the thing, you know . . . rest . . . that's what I need. Sorry to be such a poor host . . . but . . . can't be helped."

"Well, then, off with you, but I shall expect my old friend returned to me in the morning," smiled the duke, wondering what all this purported, for he had not believed the viscount for a moment.

He then found a book and attempted its pages with little success. Try as he would, his thoughts would not concentrate on the words before him. 'Twas Sir Owen's visit that had brought on the viscount's mood. He was sure of that—but why? Was Skippy involved in something to do with Celia? He had from the onset mentioned his connection with Celia . . . but he had also said that it was not known. What did it all mean? Fiend seize it all! Whereupon he retired to his room.

He threw off his blue dinner jacket and his white silk waistcoat, before going to the outside doors. Standing on the stone balcony whilst removing his cravat, he saw a dark-clad figure moving across the lawns. He leaned over the stone balustrade to get a better look and was about to call out, when he realized it was the viscount himself.

"Devil a bit!" whispered the duke to himself. "So that was it! He wanted to sneak out of the house. Why?" He watched Skippy vanish into the thicket adjoining the south lawns and felt a wretched sensation creep over him. What was Skippy up to? What was the meaning of all this? Further deliberation on the subject brought to mind the fact that he had not yet mentioned his meeting with the twins to the viscount . . . and perhaps this was just as well under the circumstances!

Morning brought a swelter of heat and a renewal of these troublesome conjectures to His Grace. He washed, shaved, and appeared at the breakfast table in a superbly cut buff-colored riding jacket and breeches. His cravat demanded admiration, as did his shining hessians, but his expression foreboded woe! However, the viscount had absented himself earlier, and the duke felt a twinge of exasperation as he bit into his toast. Well, it would appear that his questions to the viscount would have to wait—but damnation! He would get to the bottom of this mystery.

Mandy put a hand to her neck and sighed, "Oh, lud, it is sultry! Move over a bit there, Ned, you're hogging the shade!" She pushed him over forcefully and dropped down under the overhang of what was once the roof of the Abbey's chapel. "What's more . . . that dried beef was an awful breakfast, and I am so hungry. Could we not ride into Manchester and have a decent meal at an Inn? Could we not, Chauncy?"

"Coo, there now, missy. Of all the addle-brained notions! Some picture the three of us would set . . . and with the likes of Fowler nosing about!"

"But Chauncy, Mandy has a point. Manchester is too big for us to be spotted—and I'm hungry too!'

"Lord love ye, children, but I'll see what I can do," grinned Chauncy, " 'ave a fancy for a pigeon pie m'self," he said, getting up from his mound and stretching. "Think I'll go give m' Bess a song."

"Not to the house?" ejaculated Mandy fearfully.

"Ain't no fool, missy. No, I'll just catch one of the boys in the field and send him to fetch Bess to me with what we need. Now don't worry yer pretty head over it none." With that he was off to their makeshift stables.

"What would we do without Chauncy?" sighed Mandy, bringing her knee up to her chin.

"Lord, don't even want to think on it none! Demme, Mandy, but I'm fairly stalled. Think I'll go have me a walk," said Ned, standing up, "Want to come along?"

She was restless and needed the exercise, but oddly enough was loathe to leave the Abbey. "No, Ned . . . think I'll just lie about."

"Suit yourself," Ned grinned and loped off.

She watched him go, half wishing she had gone along, yet knowing she couldn't. For some inexplicable reason she had to stay behind at the Abbey. A few moments later she was gazing up into deep blue eyes, and her heart thumped traitorously within her breast. "Oh! You startled me," she said, jumping to her feet and realizing with an odd sensation that she only reached the duke's shoulder.

"Did I? I had no intention of so doing, but perhaps it may serve as a warning in the future . . . after all, it could have been anyone!"

"I should have known you would start the day out with some odious statement. 'Tis your nature, I imagine!"

"Where are Chauncy and Ned?" asked the duke, looking round, ignoring her remark but acutely aware that it nettled him.

"If you must know, Ned went for a bit of a walk, exploring, I suppose. He has a penchant for discovery," she sighed, "and Chauncy is doing what he can to procure our lunch."

"Lunch?" asked the duke surprised, " 'tis but morning."

"Ah, how astute of you to make that particular deduction, Your grace. However, we made such beasts of ourselves over our morning meal that we quite ate up all that was in our abundant larder. We are now destined for starvation unless we find a pigeon pie lurking about somewhere."

"I see," said the duke amused. His smile disturbed her in spite of herself. He saw it and attempted a truce. "Come . . . do walk with me, Amanda. I should like to discuss something with you." He offered his arm but she declined, blushing profusely and feeling stupidly missish. "No, thank you. I rather think it would present an odd picture, don't you? After all, I am masquerading as a schoolboy of sorts. What if we were spotted by some chance traveler?"

He glanced over her person, mockery once again in his bright blue eyes. She had redeposited a bullycock hat upon her golden curls and tilted it low over her face, but her figure, though slim, was most profoundly feminine. His voice went suddenly low, seductive, yet bantering and altogether charming.

"Then may I suggest . . . " his finger found the open neckline and traveled its wide open length upward to her chin, "that you don something a bit more concealing? For, my pretty gamine, your exquisite proportions quite give you away!"

Her cheeks turned a deep red, and her eyes shot darts of fire at him. This was too much—really! If he had said it with the intention of flirting, she could have given him a setdown or slapped his rakish grin off his face. But, no! He spurted off the most outrageous piece of flattery and meant it as an insult to her intelligence!

Without a word, she stopped, scooped up her dark brown buckskin waistcoat, and slipped it on, all the while silently glaring at him as he continued to appraise her. The worn vest had been her brother's when they were younger and thus it was not a bad fit, yet it did little to disguise the fact that she was a woman.

He snorted. "I suppose that will have to do. At any rate, we will walk in the thicket where I doubt we shall be seen."

"I don't suppose any impropriety can be attached to my walking alone with my guardian in the woods?" asked Mandy blithely, instinctively aware that this would irritate him.

"No more than your meeting with Sir Owen yesterday," returned the duke suavely.

She gasped with surprise. "How did you know his name? How could you know?"

"Pretty gamine . . . have I vexed you? I am not without my scope of abilities. The gentleman in question paid us a visit at Wharfedale Manor yesterday afternoon—a most unusual one, I might add."

"What do you mean?" she frowned.

"Apparently Sir Owen feels that Skip is concealing something regarding his connection with Celia," said the duke thoughtfully.

"That is absurd!" cried Mandy faithfully. "Besides— Skip had no connection with Celia!"

"That is not altogether true. Skip has himself admitted to having had a slight—rather short—intrigue with the poor girl."

Mandy gasped. "That is not true . . . it can't be true . . . Skip wouldn't . . . she was not his sort . . . I . . . I . . ."

"My dear girl, I have no notion why it should upset you so," interrupted the duke inexplicably irritated by her concern over the viscount's past interest in Celia Brinley, "but it is indeed quite true. Nevertheless, he assured me it was but a fleeting thing and over long ago. That is not the point."

"Then why mention it?"

"Because this suitor of yours seems to think it is. Sir Owen believes that Skip is cloaking his activities in such a way as to hinder Ned's chances of clearing himself."

"Sir Owen is *not* my suitor—and he is mistaken in his belief about Skippy."

"Not your suitor? He gave every indication to the contrary."

"Did he? I can't imagine why."

He put up one of his mobile black brows, but did not argue the point.

"At any rate, I feel there may be something to what he says . . . for in truth, Skip has not been himself as of late."

"But . . . it's impossible! We have known him nearly all our lives . . . he wouldn't . . . couldn't do anything to hurt Ned!"

"No, I don't think that he would intentionally . . . yet he is hiding something . . . and I mean to find out what it is." His lips suddenly set in a hard line, and his eyes held no trace of the twinkle that had danced there just moments ago.

Then Ned was coming down through the brush and waving to them. Mandy put a finger to her lips, commanding her brother to silence. He grinned when he reached them, for clearly his sister intended a rebuke.

"Oh, now, Mandy, don't scold . . . forgot I was a hunted man!"

Chapter Ten

"My dear Mrs. Brinley . . . what can I say . . . there are no words with which to console you," offered Mr. Rawlings, bending his short, wide torso low over Agatha Brinley's plump hand.

She dabbed at her eyes with her Barcelona handkerchief before swishing the air impressively with its soft black silk.

"You have no idea . . . no idea at all, Mr. Rawlings . . . what an ordeal all this has been. To lose my precious stepdaughter . . . my only child. And in such a horrific manner! And then both my dear brother's children—oh, 'tis more than I can bear!"

Since she gave every indication of succumbing to a fit of the vapors, Mr. Rawlings hastened to help her to the sofa, saying with some show of agitation, "Dreadful . . . simply dreadful . . . " As he shook his balding head in accord with his statement, it occurred to him that the matter he had come to Sherborne Halls expressly to settle with Mrs. Brinley would be a hard one to present indeed. He was just wondering how best to go about it, when Mrs. Brinley suddenly removed his state of confusion.

"But . . . we must not dwell on my tragedy." She cast a languid glance his way, indicating that he should draw up a chair beside her. As he complied, "You came here, I believe, on business."

Gratefully he pulled up his black briefcase upon his knee and brought forth a package of ivory-colored papers, speaking quickly lest the woman have a change of heart.

"Dear Mrs. Brinley . . . so good . . . so understanding. If you will but put your signature here . . ." he indicated with his quill, "and here . . . I shall not need to trouble you further."

"Indeed . . . but what am I signing?" asked the lady sharply, all semblance of grief vanished from her powdered face.

Mr. Rawlings lowered his voice. "As you know, my dear lady, your account with Barings was somewhat overdrawn and, although you sold out your funds, they were not quite enough to cover your overdraft. Oh my! This is difficult indeed! If you will but sign these, it will enable us to transfer your deceased stepdaughter's account into your own. Your solicitor assured us that you were fully aware . . . "

"Of course I am!" snapped Mrs. Brinley, glaring at the young serving girl across the room. The maid had

entered with a tray of coffee and, finding Mrs. Brinley
occupied, stood waiting so as not to disturb the conversation. Mrs. Brinley did not know how much the
girl had heard but seemed anxious that she should hear
no more. "Put the coffee down here, you silly child,
and be off!"

"Yes, mum," said the girl nervously, dropping a
curtsy.

Mrs. Brinley turned a fluttery smile upon Mr. Rawlings. "Of course, dear sir. Where did you say I should
sign?"

Mandy paced to and fro, playing fretfully with the
felt of her wide-rimmed peasant's hat. It was the hour
she had agreed to meet Sir Owen, and he was late.
When he appeared at last she greeted him enthusiastically, for she had not enjoyed waiting about in the fear
of being discovered.

"Sir Owen . . . thank goodness . . . " she half-
whispered going toward him.

He smiled in response and clasped both her small
white hands in his own large ones before she knew
what he was about. She withdrew them gently, repri-
manding him with her eyes. He laughed.

"Such a little prude, Mandy love—but that is just
as it should be. I want such a wife . . . very lovely
. . . very proper . . . "

"You are talking nonsense—and it is not that which
we should be discussing!" suggested Mandy strongly.

"No, of course, you are quite right. There will be
time enough once I have cleared Ned."

"Then you have learned something?" asked she hopefully.

"It would appear that the elusive Elly was seen some ten days ago in York. I plan to visit the fair city tomorrow and see what I can glean from her."

"Tomorrow—why not today?" cried Mandy.

"I think she will go there tomorrow for supplies. I don't think she will chance it before then from the information I have."

Mandy was amazed and so stated, "Truly, Sir Owen, you are wondrous! How is it no one else has discovered this?"

"No one else? Do you mean your groom . . . or Ned?" he asked curiously.

"No . . . I . . . I . . ." she found herself reluctant to advise him that she knew her guardian was in the vicinity. "I rather thought Skippy might have come up with some such information."

"Ah, but I have already advised you that the viscount may have reasons of his own for not wanting to find Elly," said Owen, pleased to bring home his point so neatly. She glanced away from him, but he took her chin and turned her face his way.

"Perhaps you meant your guardian . . . the Duke of Margate?" He watched her closely, "He is staying with the viscount, you know."

"I see," said Mandy carefully.

He released her, and his hazel eyes were cold, calculating. "You don't seem surprised."

"We hear things . . . even where we are," she said simply. Instinct kept her silent. "Do you think he will be of any help?"

"I'm not sure . . ." said Sir Owen thoughtfully. "He certainly has a reputation for succeeding where others have failed. But never mind him. Keep in mind what I have said about the viscount. There are reasons you should not . . . go to him. I don't think he should be told where you and Ned are hiding yourselves."

"No . . . I shan't trust anyone with that," said she quietly.

"Not even me?" he asked, coming closer.

"No, not even you. I wouldn't want you in a position where you might have to lie to the authorities," said Mandy gently.

He laughed. "A kiss, pretty Mandy—just one before I go."

"Don't be absurd," she smiled.

"When will you meet me again?" he asked, allowing this to pass.

"I . . . I don't know. But if you have a message for me . . . write it down and place it here," she said, indicating a hollow knot in a near-by oak, "and I will answer."

"So I shall, love—but I'll have that kiss," he said, bending swiftly and placing a peck upon her cherry mouth. Her hand flew up in retaliation but, before it could meet his cheek, he caught it, laughing rakishly. "That is no way to serve me for my help."

He dropped her hand with a whimsical smirk and, just as suddenly as he had arrived, he was gone. She watched him vanish among the trees before running quietly after him. She darted here and there, ducking now and then lest he catch sight of her, until at last he was by his horse and riding down the road. She watched him round the bend toward Harrowgate and was about to return to the thicket and the Abbey when a young maid walking down the road in the opposite direction caught her eye. There was something familiar about her wide ambling gait. . . .

It was an hour later when a breathless Mandy returned to the Abbey ruins. Chauncy had preceded her by a few minutes and had already distributed a bountiful array of delectables upon a woolen blanket. She dropped down unceremoniously and fell to with a squeal of delight. Her groom grinned, openly pleased with himself, as he watched her.

Unable to decide between a chicken pie and a pigeon pie, Mandy said offhandedly, "Met young Sarah from the house. She was on the way to market, and I hailed her."

"Whatever made you do such a gooseish thing?" asked her brother.

"Well . . . I trust her, you know. And I wanted to speak to her about everything up at the house. And, Ned, don't scold, because *I learned something*."

"You learned something? Now what is that supposed to signify?" inquired her brother, reaching for a strawberry tart.

" 'Tis about Aunt Agatha," said Mandy portentously, evidently feeling that all attention should be directed her way at such a moment.

"Aunt Agatha?" groaned her brother. "Faith, girl . . . not while we are eating!"

"Neddy, don't be provoking. I tell you I have learned something important about Aunt Agatha!"

"Then do . . . let us hear it," said a strong male voice behind her.

Mandy's head jerked round, and she was suddenly

aware that her heart was beating wildly. What was it about him, this cool self-composed, handsome man that aroused such feelings?

"Your Grace! I thought when you left we would not again see you till the morrow," she said with far more *sang-froid* than she felt.

"So sorry to disappoint you, but I found the viscount away from home and thought I'd drop by with a humble offering. But I see the good Chauncy has outdone me!" said the duke, bringing forth a basket of bread, cheese, and wine.

Ned fell upon the basket with enough enthusiasm to make anyone believe he had not eaten for at least twenty-four hours. He produced the wine, and handed it round, apologizing to his sister that she couldn't very well drink wine—and certainly not from a bottle.

The duke grinned and produced a single glass from the basket. "I think this particular wine mild enough for a young lady," he said. He held out the glass to Ned who filled it with a pleasant white wine. The duke then offered the glass to Amanda.

"Thank you," she managed quietly, glancing up at his face and feeling her cheeks burn beneath his smile.

"Now, tell us—what have you discovered about your aunt?" pursued the duke, taking up a position beside her on the blanket.

"She had a visitor earlier this morning," began Mandy. "Mr. Rawlings . . . of Barings Bank in York."

Her brother snorted. "What's so unusual about that? Ain't the first time the fellow has called. After all, he handles her account."

"Yes, but wait, Ned. Aunt Agatha has inherited Celia's funds—*and whatever cash Celia had in her ac-*

count!" She glanced round and found that the duke was the only one who seemed to appreciate the significance of this.

"What's that got to do with anything?" asked her brother, somewhat bewildered. " 'Tis only natural that she would—she was her stepmama—and Celia had no one else."

"But Neddy . . . don't you see? Aunt Agatha needed Celia's money. She was ruined!"

"Gadzooks!" responded her brother.

"Indeed," concurred the duke. "Ruined, you say. Had she not funds left to her from her husband?"

"They were sold out to cover her overdraft, and she was still in need of the ready, for Sarah overheard the whole, and Mr. Rawlings said that Celia's account would be transferred to cover the balance of the overdraft still remaining!"

"Coo, missy . . . that changes things a bit, don't it?" said Chauncy, seeing the light.

"Indeed it does, Chauncy!" said Mandy with no little triumph.

"Gammon!" ejaculated Ned. "If you think that Aunt Agatha stabbed her stepdaughter and then contrived to put the blame on me . . . you're out!"

"But Ned . . . you have only to see how she has taken over Sherborne Halls. Don't you see? She had access to Elly . . . she could have written that note telling you to come to the pond at seven-thirty instead of seven. She would have known you were meeting Celia . . . and she had a motive. Not only does she get Celia's money . . . she also gets Sherborne."

"I am afraid not, my dear. I believe according to the entailment of your family will, *you* would inherit the estate *in toto*," interpolated the duke quietly.

"But I am out of the way—an outlaw."

He smiled. "I doubt they would hang you for that, and when you had finished serving your internment, you would have Sherborne!"

"But she would have it in the meantime . . . and besides . . . she needed Celia's money . . . little as it is."

"Indeed, it is worth thinking about, and she did most certainly throw suspicion Ned's way . . ." said the duke thoughtfully.

Ned handed the bottle of wine to Chauncy. "Well, I don't believe it. Someone murdered poor Celia . . . but it wasn't Aunt Agatha!" Then putting up his hands as dark thoughts became too much for him, "Well, I am going fishing. Coming, Chaunce?"

"Aye, it will do us good," said the groom, standing up.

"Care to join us, Your Grace?" This from Ned.

"No, thanks. And mind you, stay out of sight."

"Of course. We have a rare spot, we do."

Mandy watched them leave, overwhelmingly aware that she was now alone with the duke. She glanced up at his face and with some chagrin noted that he seemed miles away, lost in thought.

"I take it you, too, think little of what I have discovered?" said Mandy more in the way of breaking silence than seeking his opinion, for she also doubted that Aunt Agatha had actually stabbed Celia.

"What? Oh, well, Mandy, it does not seem likely that she murdered Celia. But this Mr. Rawlings interests me. From Barings, you say?"

"Indeed, yes. Why?"

"There is something about Barings in York that nips at my memory." He then discovered her dark eyes and thought for a moment he had never before seen anything so lively and yet so soft. He felt an unnerving compulsion to reach out and caress her cheek. Restraining himself, he spoke again, "You deserve a London Season, Mandy. When we are through with this, you shall have one!"

"Shall I? You are suddenly very attentive to my needs," said Mandy, blushing slightly, for there was the trace of something she didn't understand in his voice.

"No more so than I should be . . . as your guardian." He made it sound quite abrupt. Then he rose and, flicking her nose, said more gently, "You wear that hat low, child. And keep to the Abbey . . . if not because I ask it, for your brother."

"I don't intend to do anything to hurt my brother," she answered, frowning slightly, then adding, "and I have not tried to be deliberately provoking—but I do not like being ordered about!"

"No, I don't suppose you do," he said, smiling softly. "Till later, Mandy!"

She watched him lead out his horse from the stable, and a strange sensation came over her. For a feeling of wanting him to stay had gripped her. She chided herself, "Really, you've been left to yourself too long—it is just that you are lonely—nothing more." With a force almost superhuman she put the vision of his last smile from her mind, but she was powerless to prevent her eyes from looking into her heart.

Chapter Eleven

Alfred Speenham glanced down his narrow nose and found that his pewter of ale was nearly done. He brought his languid glance up and surveyed the tavern galley of the Cock Pit with boredom. No one worth conversing with . . . and no sport to be had . . . except the wench washing down the oak tables. He called out a sally to her.

"Here now, sweetheart! Can't you see I'm fair stalled? Come sit on m'knee, and sing me a song."

"Go on wit ye, darlin'! Sing ye a song indeed! Me wit but a few hours before the evenin' rush of men. Got to keep m'strength, ye know!" rallied the plump Betty. She had no great liking for this particular gentleman, but though he was not lavish with his money, he had on occasion slipped her a coin or two.

He would have kept up a banter of sorts with her had not the tavernkeeper ordered her to the kitchen. He rose and went over to the bar with his pewter and offered it for refilling.

"Quiet this afternoon," said Speenham in way of making idle conversation.

"Aye," said the innkeeper. He did not like Speenham and made no secret of it.

"They say there is a runner staying here," suggested Speenham.

"Do they? Don't know of any . . . leastways our only guest be Mr. Fowler, and he don't call 'imself a runner."

"Then you don't believe there is anyone inquiring after the whereabouts of my cousins?"

"I don't know nought about it . . . 'ceptin' the young lord didn't no more kill that poor girl than he would his own sister!" snapped the innkeeper.

"There's some that think he did," returned Speenham carefully.

"And there's others that don't," retorted the man staunchly.

This sort of conversation could not have gone very far, and thus it was perhaps fortunate that at this particular moment a shadow filled the tavern entrance, and Speenham looked up to find an imposing figure.

"Your Grace," he hailed with a smile, pleased to exhibit his friendship with such an exalted figure before the tavernkeeper.

"Ah . . . Mr. Speenham . . ." said the duke coming forward leisurely.

"May I invite you to a bumper of ale?" He received a

condescending nod, put up two fingers, received two pewter tankards, and carried them to the table he had occupied earlier.

"What news have you of my cousins?" asked Speenham after a long pull on his tankard.

"I am afraid I have nothing to report. They have hidden themselves well. I imagine they are staying with some loyal friends."

"I would have put that as the viscount. Are you not staying there yourself? Besides, it would have leaked out, you know . . . servants . . ." said Speenham sagely.

"Undoubtedly." However, the duke's glance had shifted and found a newcomer. It was a rather short man wearing a low-crowned felt hat, an old-fashioned coat buttoned across the breast, and open over the large belly. He was hailed by the innkeeper as Mr. Fowler, but the duke felt that he would have recognized him anyway.

"Excuse me a moment," said the duke, pushing his chair back.

Speenham put out his hand, and there was a strange expression in his eyes.

"What the deuce do you think you are doing?"

"Why, I am going to go have a word with Mr. Fowler. I understand he is new to Yorkshire and is looking to buy property," said the duke, raising a brow to indicate he would have no interference.

"But Your Grace," whispered Speenham, "I . . . I think the fellow is a runner."

"Indeed? I am quite certain of it," smiled the duke as he gave Alfred Speenham his back. "Mr. Fowler," he said, with an utterly charming smile, "won't you join Mr. Speenham and myself at our table?"

"Eh? How did ye know m'calling, and who might *ye* be?" asked Mr. Fowler. He was a suspicious man by nature, made more so by his profession.

The duke inclined his head: "I am Brock Haydon, Duke of Margate. And I have heard that you are looking for land in the vicinity. As it happens, a friend of mine has a parcel that he is thinking of putting up for sale . . . ."

"Is that so? Well, Yer Grace . . ."

"Come . . . do sit with us so that we may be private," interrupted the duke in his most gracious manner.

"Thankee . . . think I will," replied the runner, taking up a chair and sinking heavily upon its stiff wood seat. The duke procured a tankard of ale for the man and took up a chair beside him, noting that Speenham looked uncomfortable. His brow went up, but he said nothing to this.

Mr. Fowler took a long pull of ale before setting his pewter mug down.

"There now, you say this friend of yers has some land?"

"Indeed yes, several acres," said the duke.

"May I know his name . . . this friend of yers?"

"Of course, though I must caution you that this is most confidential."

Mr. Fowler acknowledged this by nodding. Mr. Speenham said nothing.

"It is the Viscount Skippendon's land. Though I am not familiar with the terms, I do believe the price may be most attractive," suggested the duke blandly.

"Is that so? Well, I am most particular about what I want. Looking for something near water."

"Just so. His land borders the Wharfedale River, you know," offered the duke enthusiastically.

"Well, well . . . I'm looking for just such a spot. When I'm ready, I shall be happy to approach him, I will. But for now, I think I'll jest keep looking."

"For . . . for what?" Mr. Speenham asked, finding his voice at last.

"For what I am really interested in," said Mr. Fowler looking directly at him. Then he glanced up and discovered a man holding a hat in his hand. He was elderly with a balding head, respectably attired, and apparently there by appointment. Mr. Fowler put up his hand. "Ah, Mr. Rawlings." He turned to his host, "If ye will excuse me . . . I 'ave an appointment. . . ."

"Of course," said the duke, still smiling. He watched Mr. Fowler lead Mr. Rawlings out of the tavern galley and up the Inn stairs, presumably to his room.

What in damnation did a Bow Street runner want with Mr. Rawlings of Barings Bank? Unless Mandy's earlier supposition had some truth in it. Could Aunt Agatha have had something to do with Celia's murder? And what was it nagging his thoughts . . . something about Barings Bank . . . something he had read in the *Chronicle* weeks ago.

"Why on earth did you invite him over here?" asked Mr. Speenham, breaking in on the duke's thoughts.

"Why? I thought it clear . . . he's looking for land—I offered him some," said the duke with intent.

"You know as well as I that he is a runner—after my cousins," snorted Speenham.

"Yes, I do believe he is a runner. Why are you suddenly so concerned?"

"After all, one doesn't want one's own cousins captured by a London runner."

"Indeed—when it was your own father who turned Ned in to the authorities for questioning?"

"That was a thing quite different," said Mr. Speenham sullenly.

"Was it indeed? I fail to see the difference. Goodday, sir." The duke pushed his chair back suddenly to take his leave. He had just about as much as he could stomach of Speenham's face—and he needed to think.

As he mounted his black, a familiar figure on horseback approached him.

"Margate!"

He eyed Sir Owen unsmilingly and nodded, "Goodafternoon, sir."

"Are you returning to Wharfedale Manor?" He received a curt nod from the duke and, ignoring this coldness, continued unperturbed. "I am myself returning to my house—and as our paths are for a time the same, I thought we might talk along the way."

"Not, sir, if your conversation carries some of yesterday's strain," said the duke stiffly.

Ever pleasant when it suited his purpose, Sir Owen chuckled.

"Come now. You can't think me such a rum-touch. What I had to say . . . I said to Skippendon's face . . . not his back! Now admit it, Margate, you can have no quarrel with me on that score, and there is something I should like to discuss with you."

"Indeed?" said the duke unpleasantly. He had no liking for Sir Owen. Admittedly the fellow would have been a jolly companion in the revelry of London, but somehow, here in the openness of Yorkshire, things took on a different hue. "But agreed, it would be foolish to ride without the common courtesy of idle conversation." He looked penetratingly at Sir Owen. "What did you wish to discuss with me?"

"Amanda Sherborne," said Sir Owen in a tone that brought the heat to the duke's head—and something else to mind.

"I see. What about Miss Sherborne?" It also occurred to him that if any man was capable of seducing a pretty maid, Sir Owen was, and . . . *Miss Celia had been seduced.*

"She is your ward, and therefore I thought it . . . not expedient but polite to inform you that I intend to marry her," said Owen blandly.

"Because you stand in need of a fortune?"

"I find that I am overly fond of Miss Sherborne and that her inheritance is not something to be ignored!"

"Do you seek my approval? If so, you are out Owen. Mark me, I would stand in your way!" snorted the duke.

"I don't need your approval, Margate! If the lady will have me—and she will, I will take her. She comes of age in a month or so. My creditors can wait, . . . though I have a horse running soon, and chances are in my favor," he said thoughtfully.

"Of all the brazen fellows!" sneered the duke, feeling hot as fire. "I doubt Miss Sherborne is such that she won't see through you!"

"You are quite out there. Mandy welcomes my

suit," said Owen artfully. He suspected that the duke knew Amanda and Ned's whereabouts, and he was determined to discover if he were in the right of it.

"Does she indeed? Then do I take it, you have managed to court the lady whilst she is in hiding?"

"Everyday, duke, every day. Why, only this morning, we discussed our future." Sir Owen saw the duke as an opponent in many respects. He observed the duke's growing irritation and wondered at it. Was it possible that the duke had not only been with his wards but had found the little Amanda desirable? Was it jealousy he was arousing? This was serious, for he needed Mandy for himself. The immediate future held the certainty of funds, of that he had made sure. But Mandy's inheritance would make him easy for the rest of his days. He added lightly, "Did not Amanda tell you of . . . ?" He was fishing but came up with nothing. The duke had already collected himself.

"Tell me?" he cut him off sharply. "How could she possibly tell me? I thought you realized that I have not yet met my wards!"

"Really? They have not managed to send you word as to their whereabouts?"

"No. I have heard nothing from them."

Owen digested this quietly. They reached a narrow turn-off in the road, and he smiled once again, "Goodday to you, Margate, this is where I leave you."

The duke nodded a dismissal rather than a farewell and proceeded down the pike. His temper was scarcely in check and bits of embers were still seething within his soul. There was absolutely no logic to it, yet he wanted to get to Mandy, face her, and find out just how far advanced was her relationship with the profligate Sir Owen. God! but she had lied to him . . . and so innocently!

He reached the Abbey ruins some twenty minutes later and managed to stable his horse without coming upon her. By the time he found her beneath the shade of a near-by evergreen, his wrath had exploded.

"What the devil do you think you are doing?" he shouted.

She raised her exquisitely piquant face, and her dark eyes were filled with surprise. Her bright hair had fallen around her face and shoulders, and she brushed it aside as she answered, "Whatever is wrong?"

"By God, girl! Are you a fool? Why don't you just announce your whereabouts to the world at large and end the matter?"

"Have you lost your mind? How dare you speak to me in such a fashion!" she snapped, her own quick temper unleashed.

"How dare I? I am your guardian—and Ned's, and it is my considered opinion that you have set yourself and your brother in grave jeopardy by your thoughtless behavior!"

"My thoughtless . . ." said the lady getting to her feet and wheeling round to face him, "I can't believe I am hearing correctly. I was well hidden from the road . . . no one travels through this particular glen—'tis haunted, you know—and . . . good Lord! Am I not allowed *some* freedom?"

"It would appear that you take it whether it is permitted or not!"

She could not think what had come over him. Earlier that afternoon he had gone a fair way toward ingratiating himself in her heart, and now suddenly he was transformed into a devil.

"What is wrong?" she repeated. "What has happened? And why are you raging at me in this manner? Surely not because I chose to read my book beneath a tree some hundred feet from the Abbey?"

"That, my wide-eyed gamine, my innocent," he sneered, "is nothing to your duplicity! But come, let us have a sampling of what you give others so freely," said the duke, suddenly aware that he had to take her in his arms. The sight of her burned him in more ways than he had ever imagined possible. His hands clasped her to him roughly as his mouth sought hers.

It was all she ever dreamed a kiss could be. Intense emotion swept through her veins until she felt herself go limp in his embrace. She had to remind herself that she loathed this savage libertine, that he was misusing her. However, the state of her heart seemed to contradict such thoughts. She had to raise her hands and forcibly strike at his shoulders. And then, suddenly he was flinging her away from him, as though he no longer had use for her—no longer wanted that which he had taken. She gasped with the release and, had she had will and thoughts intact, would have stormed at him in a violent tirade. But he had already turned on his heel and stalked away.

A madman! Of course—there is no other explanation for it—he is a madman! She thought to herself as she watched him vanish. Her next realization was the indisputable fact that her body trembled uncontrollably with the vivid memory of his touch and that his kiss, though brutal, engendered a turbulent sensation in her own breast.

Chapter Twelve

For a time His Grace rode at a reckless pace, taking the long route home, for he had to sort out his thoughts. Hell and brimstone! The dark-eyed Mandy had him fairly winded—and he knew not how or why. He was conscious only that for a moment he had wanted to shake her—and then to kiss her. And kiss her he certainly had. There was, he told himself, no excuse for such unpardonable behavior. He had played the cad—and she must think him a scoundrel. Indeed, at that particular moment, he thought himself little better than one.

What right had he? None, he answered himself, none at all. As her guardian, he should direct. But instead, he had found himself the seducer—forcing a kiss upon his own ward. Yet he knew that when he held her body against his, he had no proper feelings. Her sweet, honeyed lips were like no other woman's— and he had wanted to go on kissing her. In fact, it denoted something of the duke's strength of character and will that he had not continued to satisfy so heady a desire. For a moment he thought he was lost. Somehow, he knew not by what process, she had taken hold of his thoughts, weaving her way into his own needs. He saw her not as a child, though he tried, but as a desirable, untamed woman. He attempted to dispel such notions by constantly treating her as the gamine he had dubbed her, but it had not worked.

The duke had not reached the age of twenty-seven and still maintained his freedom by falling victim to pretty faces and wild spirits. He had every intention of retaining his bachelor status and consoled himself that as soon as he had freed the twins from their predicament, he would return to London and find a beauty to wipe away all memory of Amanda Sherborne. He had no doubt this ingenious method he had discovered in his youth would work. It always had in the past, it should in the future, and yet . . .

"Bah!" said the duke aloud as he turned down the drive of Viscount Skippendon's estate. A light drizzle had started, and he whipped up his horse into a canter. He wanted company now. That was what he needed, good brandy and jovial spirits.

When he came upon Skip in the library some ten minutes later, he rather thought that here now was the company, but certainly not the jovial spirits he stood in need of! The viscount stood before the glass garden

doors gazing out upon the wet roses, thoughtfully pulling at his lower lip. He heard the duke's approach and
turned his head, "Brock! So you are back, are you?
Where the deuce have you been?"

"Where have *I* been?" returned the duke, his eyes
twinkling. "You're wonderful, Skip. You have contrived to be gone from your house more hours than you
have spent in it, and you want to know where *I* have
been! Demme, but that is doing it brown!"

The viscount grinned.

"I've been with m'solicitors today . . . had a
bit . . . well, never mind that. Tell me what's toward. When you first walked in here, had the devil in
your eye. I'd swear to it, so no use trying to bamboozle
me, old friend."

"Ha! It would serve you if I gave what I've been
getting, but no, I'm a better friend than that!" bantered
the duke, dropping down upon the sofa. "However
much you deserve to be kept in the dark, I beg leave
to tell you that I have met both my wards some two
nights ago!"

"What?" exclaimed the viscount, coming forward.
"Where . . . how?"

"I was in fact held up by them on the main pike
and nearly blew a hole through Amanda Sherborne's
pretty little head!"

The viscount felt it encumbent upon himself to
take a seat. He did, his mouth agape as he whispered,
"Upon my soul . . ."

"I would have, had it been otherwise. It was *you*
they were trying to cut a wheedle with, m'bucko.
Totally confounded when I stepped out of your car-

riage, and if I hadn't thought Miss Sherborne too fair and ageless a youth to die . . . well . . ."

"But . . . but . . ." tried the viscount, "she is a girl."

"I did not find that out until a few moments later when we came to fisticuffs!" said the duke, pleased to be astounding his friend.

"This is . . . most shocking!" breathed the viscount.

"Exactly what I was brought home to realize. Ever since that night I have been at odds to set things to rights for those two . . . but it won't be easy!" sighed the duke.

"But . . . but how has all this happened without a word to me?"

"You were not around to hear any of it, Skip," said the duke, rather stiffly bringing home a point. The viscount blushed.

"Er . . . yes . . . but there were reasons . . . never mind that now, finish the tale, you dog!"

"You have the gist of it, my friend. What more do you want?"

"You can't leave it at that! Demme! What did you think of your wards? Where are they? What have they been doing?"

"What did I think? I thought them a wholesome pair. Ned should do, when his lease of infancy is at an end—yes, he will do. Right sort, you know."

"And Amanda . . . she is well?"

He frowned. "She is in excellent health—and spirits." Then, pausing a moment, "Tell me, Skippy, does she have a *tendre* for Sir Owen?"

Skip snorted. "Mandy ain't a fool for all her hoyden ways. Sir Owen may be casting out lures, but I'd as lief think she would drown before reaching his way!"

"That is a bit strong. You mustn't think she don't have eyes for the fellow simply because you find *yourself* at outs with him."

"Ain't that! Told you, Brock, she is no fool. Green, yes, how could she be otherwise stuck up here in the wilds? Ain't up to snuff, but her head is squarely upon her shoulders, and she sees him for what he is. Lord, she knows the difference between an engaging rascal like yourself, and a park-sauntering gamster!"

"And Sir Owen is a . . . park-sauntering gamster?" laughed the duke, much amused.

"Precisely," said Skip unrelentingly.

"And how would you define yourself?" sallied the duke.

"A right'un, and well you know it!" retorted the viscount, his vague eyes brimming with laughter.

"Well, then, what has you looking so glum? And don't pitch anymore gammon at me about headaches and such!" commanded the duke suddenly.

The viscount's smile vanished. "You don't want a round tale, then don't be asking me any questions. Look, Brock, you are my closest . . . dearest . . . most valued friend . . ." He waited as the duke inclined his head, the smirk of a smile well hidden. The viscount noted it and took umbrage. "Well, you *are*. But what you can do for me this time . . . well, you can't . . . and it ain't something I can tell. Leave it at that, Brock."

It was obvious that his friend was in earnest. Dissatisfied but willing to accommodate him at the present time, the duke allowed the matter to drop. "Very well then, let me bring you up to date with regard to the twins. There is a runner in town staying at the Cock Pit. Oh, by the by, I offered to sell him a parcel of your land—the section bordering the Wharfe River," said the duke, his eyes lively.

"You did what?"

"So sorry, old boy. He didn't seem very interested in the deal," returned the duke glibly.

"He didn't want it?" blustered the viscount, torn between wrath over having his beloved land rejected and his indignation at the duke for offering it up to a Bow Street runner.

"What the devil do you mean, he didn't want it? 'Tis some of the finest property in all of Yorkshire! Confound you anyway, Brock, how dare you go about the countryside putting up my land for sale! I don't want to sell it . . . any of it. And what's more, I won't sell it!" exploded the viscount, much incensed.

The duke laughed and slapped his friend's knee. A footman had arrived with a tray of tea and sweetcakes. The two gentlemen waited until this had been set on the coffee table between them, the tea poured, and the footman gone, before resuming the conversation. The duke rose, strode over to the brandy decanter, and brought it to their tea, whereupon he dropped a bit of the firewater into their cups and handed one to his friend.

"There now, Skip," he attempted to placate him.

"No use coming on sweet! I won't sell m'land. I tell you I *won't!*"

"I have no intention of allowing you to do so,"

offered the duke, finding that his friend would need some calming down before they could proceed.

"You don't?" asked Skip, eying the duke suspiciously.

"No, I don't. Rest easy, Skip. You see the runner, Mr. Fowler he calls himself, is posing as a cit on holiday and looking to buy some local color. Offered him yours as a way of introducing myself and nosing him out."

"Nosing him out? Oh, my God!" said the viscount, suddenly seeing the light, "is he here after Ned?"

"That is the odd part of it all. I can't fathom his purpose, though we must assume that is precisely why he is here."

"Well? What happened?" asked the viscount impatiently.

"Nothing. A gentleman from Barings Bank in York came in and . . . hold a moment!" said the duke, putting down his cup. "My God! Now I know what it is that has been bothering me. Of course!" He rose to his feet and started across the room.

"Devil a bit!" ejaculated the viscount. "Where the deuce do you think you are going?"

"To the Cock Pit to see Mr. Fowler," returned the duke.

Skippy picked up a small iced cake and slipped it into his mouth. "Well! I think it is all too smoky by half! Bow Street runners wanting to buy my land! Don't like it! What's more, won't sell it . . . not an inch! Crazy fellow, Brock, forever getting involved in such dealings. Well, I won't be a party to it. 'Tis my land after all!"

The duke's horse was not particularly pleased to have the additional exercise and complained obstinately as the duke set out for town. He commanded his stallion authoritatively and tightened his hold on the reins before he was able to settle the stallion into obedience. At last he was on his way through the mist to the Cock Pit, thoroughly excited about what he had remembered.

He could see the lights of the tallow candles as he approached the tavern and dismounted as the ostlers rushed out to take charge of his horse. Although in the early afternoon the tavern had been almost deserted, it was now inundated with gentlemen in festive spirits. The duke doffed his hat to a buxom wench and grasped her by the arm.

"Can you direct me to Mr. Fowler's room?"

"Aye, that I can, sir—unless you have a change of 'eart and want m'own." She smiled broadly at him, for such a flash cove was just what she liked.

He grinned boyishly. "Perhaps another time. Mr. Fowler, please."

She sighed, "Aye, first room at the top of the steps." He took hold of the wooden railing and managed the steps two at a time, until he reached the landing and Mr. Fowler's door, where he knocked.

" 'Tis open! Come in if ye wish!" said the voice on the other side.

The duke opened wide the door and inclined his head, "Mr. Fowler?"

"Aye, Yer Grace. Back are ye? Well, come in, and be seated," said the runner getting up to offer a chair.

The duke went into the room and closed the door behind him. He removed his long black cape and his hat, before seating himself on a wooden chair.

"I believe in playing with a full deck, sir, so I shall come right to the point. You are not on holiday, and you are not looking for land."

"No? Then what am I doing?" asked Mr. Fowler cautiously.

"You, Mr. Fowler, are a Bow Street runner," he picked up a small black book labeled 'occurrence ledger' before Joe Fowler could stop him and dropped it again on the table, "and you are in Yorkshire looking for the fifty thousand pounds in gold that was stolen over six weeks ago!"

Joe Fowler heaved a long sigh and scanned the duke's face. "Well now, ain't ye a knowing one?" He rubbed his round chin. "It's a queer fetch—no denying that— but what a flash covey sech as yerself wants in it is more than I can prig!"

"I have my reasons for wanting to lend you my assistance," said the duke carefully.

"Aye, I dessay ye do, seeing as ye be guardian to that Sherborne lad."

The duke looked startled a moment before he recovered. "So, you know about His Lordship's trouble?"

"I ain't here on that particular setout. Lor' bless ye, gent, I don't mean to tangle wit more than I can 'andle, and this 'ere is 'arder than most would think!"

"Yes, if I recall correctly, nothing was ever heard about the guards and the drivers . . . no trace of the coach?"

"Aye, we got it down that one of them guards had

to be in on it, coz he spoke peculielike to his missus before he left that night. Could be wrong about him, but it do make sense!"

"Did it ever cross your mind that the two incidents— the theft of the gold and the death of Celia Brinley— might be related?" asked the duke cautiously.

"No, but if that be so, then the young lord be in fer a time of it. But I'll tell ye wot. That Mr. Rawlings of the Barings Bank—'twas his bank that was twigged, you know . . ."

"Yes, I know," interrupted the duke, nodding his head. "I read a small article about it at the time. Something about the exchange of paper currency for the newly minted gold . . ."

"Aye, Barings was sending a delivery to their branch over in Manchester . . . when poof! no coach, no drivers, no guards. Queer start that . . . till I got up here and went over the route. There's that river—the Wharfe . . . heard tell how there might be limestone canyons hidden from sight in these parts. Could be the coach was sunk afterwards. Could be those poor coves was buried."

"And you have nothing to go on?"

"Not anything to get m'teeth into, though I did gleam something this afternoon."

"What?" asked the duke. The sound of quiet power in his tone was such that it put Joe Fowler in the way of trusting him, yet he hesitated.

"Now, ho, there a moment, Yer Grace. Ye be quality right and tight. But who's to give me leave to go telling ye sech as that?"

"Your instincts, Joe . . . trust your instincts. Together, we may piece the puzzle. There isn't a soul in the area that doesn't know you are a runner. You'll never learn a thing from them, but I might!"

Joe Fowler cast his small round eyes over the duke's face.

"There be more truth in that than ye know, gent. Well, then, I'm going to give ye what I 'ave on this 'ere rig . . . see if two 'eads can't make sense of it."

"Good Joe! Now about Mr. Rawlings and what he said to lend substance to my fancy that Celia's death had something to do with this gold robbery?"

"Aye. Well, to give it in a bundle wrapped all neat, it's this way, Yer Grace. He let it slip that he told Mrs. Brinley about the shipment—sparing no details, such was her interest. Never thought nought about it again. Seems the old fidget likes to gab. He never said a word about his slip before . . . afeard to lose his position at the bank . . . and he says he didn't think it made a haporth o' difference."

"So that was it? Of course! It fits! Now, Joe, why don't you tell me what Rawlings told Mrs. Brinley?"

"Eh?"

"Just exactly what was the route, the time of day, all the sordid details of the fatal shipment?"

Chapter Thirteen

It was over dinner that Mandy parted with some information, a move she was to regret later. She was sitting with her brother and groom at the small table in the confines of their underground chamber. A buckskin jacket round her shoulders warded off the dampness the mist had brought to the air. She picked at her freshly caught trout dinner without enthusiasm, saying idly, "Met with Sir Owen today, Neddy."

"What? Good Lord, Mandy! Are you daft?" ejaculated her brother. "However came that about? Didn't the duke tell you to stay put?"

"If you are going to take on so . . . " said Mandy, taking affront rather more quickly than was her wont, "I won't tell you what Sir Owen was decent enough to tell me!" She stayed in position, giving him a challenging glance for she was in no mood to submit to abuse, feeling keenly that she had had enough for one day.

"*I* ain't bickering at ye, missy," offered Chauncy, picking at his teeth with a thin splint of wood. He gave her a wide open smile, hoping for one in return. Something was wrong with the girl. He sensed it, yet couldn't define it. All he could do was try to ease her back into spirits.

She was rarely proof against Chauncy. "I shall gladly tell *you*—but I do think Ned should leave the room!"

"I will not!" retorted her brother, feeling himself ill used. He folded his arms and put up a stubborn chin.

"Oh, stay then, but don't be nipping at me again, Ned," she warned. "Sir Owen was kind enough to offer his help, and I accepted—on your behalf as well as my own. You should be grateful!"

"And so I am—just think you ought to listen to the duke," said her brother by way of explanation. "Said you weren't to leave the Abbey—and the duke is a knowing sort of fellow."

He had no way of knowing this particular form of reasoning would goad her into further fury and was a bit surprised by her strange attitude.

She found the power to control herself, merely casting him a darkling glance and saying between clenched teeth, "Do you—or do you *not*—want to hear what passed between Sir Owen and myself?"

"We do," put in Chauncy hastily. " 'Tis that anxious we are, missy, so give us the lay of it."

"Very well," said Mandy condescendingly. "It seems Sir Owen has received information pertaining to Elly

Bonner. He believes that she may be in York tomorrow or some time thereafter."

"York—tomorrow?" exclaimed Ned. "Why?"

"I'm not too clear on that . . . wondered about it myself . . . but Sir Owen seems to think it will be about time she should be going in for supplies. It seems she was in York some ten days ago. . . ."

"Good Lord!" Ned jumped up from his wooden seat. "Come on, Chaunce," he said, reaching for his floppy peasant hat and planting it firmly on his flaxen curls.

"Now hold there, laddie," started Chauncy, "what do ye think ye be doing bouncing up like that?"

"Don't you see, Chauncy? This could mean that Hawkins frequents York! I know an excellent fellow—works at the Bull & Pen Tavern in York—and if anyone would know whether that brute Hawkins has been in, he would."

Chauncy flicked his own nose, acceding this to be a point. He stood up and bidding Mandy good-bye, followed His Lordship out of the chamber. Mandy called after them, but as they failed to answer her, she threw down her fork and uttered a very unladylike exclamation.

They saddled their mounts and led them out of the makeshift stable into the open air. Chauncy cast his eyes upward and felt the cool air touch his face. A bright moon glowed in the night sky and he grunted with approval, "Macfarlane's Lantern! It bodes well!"

"Eh? Whose lantern?" queried Ned with interest. Chauncy had ever a habit of lapsing into such terms, and there was sure to be a curious tale connected with them.

"Macfarlane's. Haven't I never told ye aboot it?" He

received a shake of His Lordship's head and an urging to proceed with the tale. " 'Twas the Clan Macfarlane that rode the highlands. Aye, but 'twas glorious! When the moon be so lit . . . 'tis said they would ride on their excursions and on no other time."

"So a full moon is a Macfarlane Lantern?" asked Ned laconically summing it up.

"Aye."

"Well, then, if the clan is with us, let us ride," grinned Neddy.

"Aye," agreed his groom unhesitantly, "but, m'lord, ye'll be pleased to remember yer thieves' cant ain't never been what it should. 'Twould be best to keep yer mum closed. I'll do the jawing!"

"Chauncy!" returned Ned, real hurt in his tone. "I can sport cant with the best of them!"

"Can ye now? I seem to remember it different. Or maybe ye was confusing yerself wit yer sister?"

His Lordship blushed, opened his mouth to retort, thinking his groom had taken a bit too much license with such an unjust remark. However, he then thought it better suited his dignity to ride out ahead and give Chauncy a taste of silence. This he did and was somewhat chagrined to hear his groom's booming laughter behind him.

Mandy, alone in her chamber, attempted many things to while away the hours. At first she tried reading, but found she could not concentrate on the words. She picked up her brush and went to work on her hair, but this proved tedious in the extreme. There was nothing for it but to sleep. She undressed and slipped on her muslin nightdress and stretched out on her linen-covered straw. There she lay, her eyes tightly shut, but wide awake. She endured this for a time before giving it up. She lit a tallow, glanced at her timepiece and was startled to find it was well near midnight. This was insufferable. Where were they? Really, York was no more than an hour's ride away, and they had been gone for hours and hours.

Impetuosity got the better of her, and it was not long before she was once again fully dressed. She pulled on her buckskin riding jacket and, with a determination born of frustration, she made her way up the jagged stone steps to her horse. She had her mare saddled and was up on its back before she even knew what she intended. She only knew she couldn't bear the waiting any longer.

A light mist was hugging the ground, but Mandy had not lived on the moors nearly all her life without coming across such a phenomenon before. She attached no unearthly cause to the light gray tentacles at her horse's hocks. She crossed Bolton Glen to the main pike, taking this eastward for a short stretch before crossing it and turning onto a path that etched its way through the viscount's river property. It was a shortcut she knew that would eventually put her on the Old Track to York. The fact that the branches of the trees hung over the path making grotesque shadows did not deter her. She knew the woods well and thought nothing of guiding her horse through its dark, winding overgrowths. It was a distance to York and treacherous going at night through such terrain, but Mandy kept her fears hidden from herself.

Then she was out of the woods and pleased to find the moon free above and lighting the moors before her.

The scent of heather filled her nostrils and calmed her alarm. She urged her mare through the low rolling sway of land until she came to a stretch of moor she had never before taken at night. It was known as Witch's Elbow and was avoided even during the day because of the tales told concerning it. As she drew in her breath, heaved it out, and gently urged her horse on to its treacherous ground, she came to her senses!

A sobbing! It sounded like a woman . . . yet it did not sound human. But there was no denying the strength of tone, and it seemed to be all around. She shuddered and remembered how Chauncy had warned them against Witch's Elbow.

" 'Tis the spirits of evil caught beneath its ground— make no mistake! And they cry for release, they do. 'Specially when the moon be full!"

She had been only a child then and eagerly asked how the witches had been caught beneath that stretch of moors. Chauncy had laughed.

"Why, it was wise old Saltersgash! Back in 1750, he had an inn that the witches used to play their tricks upon. So, he fixed 'em up right and tight. Tricked 'em into a bog, and built a hearth above it. Never let the fire go out. Tis there still—called the Witches' Room. When ye be old enough, with yer Grandfather's permission, that is—I'll be taking ye to it, to clap yer poppers on!"

They had exclaimed with delight at the thought of the expedition, but somehow it had been forgotten. Mandy was pragmatic, even in an age when it was rare to be so. Yet, though she knew there was a logical basis for the eerie noises going round her head, it did not come to mind at the moment. Wind? No, there were no trees for the wind to whip and make a stir. What then? She could come up with no solution and, though no coward, she felt suddenly that she was being quite foolish riding all the way to York. To what purpose? She could not go into the Bull & Pen . . . and perhaps by now, Chauncy and Neddy were back at the Abbey.

Rationalization came to her rescue, and she turned her horse about without the least bit of guilt. Really, she was sure Ned and Chauncy would be back at the Abbey—and most worried about her. She made for Wharfedale Manor woods where she took the path heading southerly towards her own Abbey glen. She spoke quietly to her horse, steadying its gait down to a brisk walk, ducking her head low to avoid the overhanging branches. Then, quite suddenly, the breeze brought not only the scent of the lush damp woods, but the sound of human conversation. It was low, hurried, and very, very near.

Mandy tried not to breathe as she listened. She heard not only her own intake and release of air but that of her horse as well. She was sure the mare's light snorting would be heard and slipped off its back and went to the reins. She covered the horse's mouth with her scarf and cooed gently, "Hush now sweet thing . . . sshhh." She walked it a pace, but as the sounds grew nearer, she led her mare into the thicket and stopped, fearful of being seen.

The voices seemed louder, and one sounded strangely familiar. Curiously, she wondered who it was stealing about in Skippy's forest preserve. Poachers? 'Twas an odd hour indeed for such activity. She picked through the bushes, gingerly bracing herself behind a thick oak, for although she could not see anyone, their voices came clearly to her ears.

"My dearest, this cannot continue. I won't have you riding out in the midst of the night . . . alone just for a few stolen moments together." It was a desperate male voice, and it was well known to Amanda Sherborne, for it belonged to Viscount Skippendon.

A soft, sweet-sounding female voice answered his anguish, and her tone was gentle, loving, and slightly accented. Irish, thought Mandy, hearing the hint of a melodious brogue. "But they are precious moments, m'darlin'. Don't take on so . . . 'tis only a wee bit more we shall have to deal with. Soon . . . soon we will be able to . . ."

Skippendon cut her off, his voice sharp, unhappy. "No! My only love . . . it must stop . . . now! That is, unless you feel we can . . ."

He stopped, as though silenced by a gloved finger. "My sweet John! Darling, you will not deny me our moments together. Tis *your* right to claim so much more . . . but I canna give it yet . . . though 'tis my wish."

"But why? Oh God! This is torture, Kathline . . . ."

"But you know why . . . have known . . . though you never really understood. But whist there, darling . . . never mind! My John!" Mandy imagined the woman reaching up to give him her lips.

But at this juncture, she had heard enough and felt like a spy. She had to control her feet, restrain them from ravaging the underbrush in her haste to reach her horse and be gone. She scrambled onto her mare, urging her out of the thicket and back onto the path. They

could not see her from where they were, though they
might hear her horse's hooves. But she didn't care.
She had to get away . . . and wished she hadn't heard
what had passed. It made her feel every bit a traitor
to the friendship she had always had with John Skippendon. Her own Skippy . . . meeting a woman
clandestinely . . . why? The woman was unknown to
her, yet she was sure she was Quality. But what was
she doing sneaking out into the night to meet with
Skip? Who could she be? She was Irish though the
accent was nearly hidden with that soft refined voice.
But, faith, what did it mean?

Then suddenly, the nagging feeling that had been
pushing itself forward, welled up over her. Sir Owen
had said Skip was seeing a woman—he had said so
many things about him—insinuating that Skip and
Celia had been lovers. He had said such ugly things,
and she had refused to hear . . . refused to believe.
Oh, God! Was Skip the father of Celia's unborn child?

A tear rose to Mandy's dark eyes and spilled over.
She heard Sir Owen's voice repeating that Skip was not
to be trusted. A man she had trusted nearly all her
life had suddenly become . . . a stranger. Skip might
have been Celia's lover, hence, he might have been the
father . . . might have murd . . . oh, no, not Skip!
Over and over these fancies taunted her until the tears
overflowed in force, staining her cheeks, blurring her
vision. It couldn't be Skip. Yet some of what Sir Owen
had said was true. Skip was involved secretly with an
unknown woman.

She had to cross the main pike which weaved
through the viscount's estate and Bolton Glen. As she
hurried her horse across, she sniffled and dabbed at her

eyes with her hands. As a result of this, she saw only what was directly before her, the road and the glen for which she aimed. She neither saw nor heard the figure on horseback coming directly at her, on his return journey from the Harrowgate Cock Pit!

He was darkly clad in his cape. His hat was pulled low, rakishly, over his eyes. He was in deep thought, but though Mandy was some two hundred feet away, the slowness with which she discerned the road before her gave him ample time to survey her. Her hat flopped about her face, but the moonlight lit upon the cheek and the pert nose. There too, there was something in the way she sat her horse. Rarely had he seen such an excellent seat on a horsewoman. Her shoulders were well laid back, with gentle grace, her head . . . just so. He felt he would have known her were they in the black of night! He called out her name and quickened his trot until he was upon her and reaching for her reins.

She saw him and balked, ashamed that he should find her alone on the road and tear-stained. She pulled the reins from him and sent her horse into a canter. The Abbey glen was reached, with the duke just behind her. It occurred to him that she had been out, meeting with someone. Whom—Sir Owen? The thought caused him pain, but he made up his mind to it and followed. They had nearly reached the abbey before he managed to bring her horse to a halt. His voice was like a strap across her cheeks. "Damnation, girl! What the devil do you mean taking off like that? And where the deuce have you been?"

She lifted her eyes, no longer in a mood to fight. The tears still flowed freely and, though she checked the sob in her throat, her state of anguish did not allow her to speak. Nor did her condition pass unnoticed by His Grace.

He jumped off his horse and came round, lifting her off hers, saying gently, worry in his voice, "Mandy, what has overset you . . . please do tell me."

"Oh, Your Grace, 'tis Skip . . . 'tis Skip . . ." cried Mandy, going into his arms and crying against the firmness of his chest. Forgotten was this afternoon. Gone was his earlier strange behavior. All she knew was that he was here . . . and that she needed him.

"Come," he said, bringing one arm around her slim shoulders and leading her gently. His free hand held the reins of both horses as he brought them to the Abbey ruins. As they walked, she poured all her tears and sobs into the crook of his arm and, when he thought she had done, he produced his handkerchief and offered it to her. She took it gratefully, dabbed at her eyes, wiped her cheeks, blew her nose, thanked him, and offered to return the abused cloth to him, however the offer was graciously declined. This produced a musical if somewhat unsteady giggle, and an absurdly pleasant sensation ran through him at the sound.

"There now, little gamine. Perhaps you feel sufficiently recovered to put me in the way of understanding what it is about our amiable Skippy to set you to tears?" There was a twinkle in his eye, but it did not belie the concern in his voice.

She needed no further prodding and immediately repeated to him what she had heard in the viscount's sylvan setting just moments ago. The duke frowned over this but said nothing until she was done.

"What do you think it means?" she cried, hoping that he would have a reasonable answer.

"It means that you certainly should not be out late and by yourself. Just look at the problem you have caused yourself. There is an explanation, you know. It is just that we don't have it readily at hand. Why don't you go below and wash your face, while I set your horse for the night?"

She acquiesced without demur and left him above-stairs. She washed, brushed out her hair, and sat down to await his coming. There were questions bothering at her, but then the sound of her brother's laughter brought her to her feet and even lighted up her face.

Chapter Fourteen

"By Jove, we've had a rare kick-up!" said Ned as he ducked his head and entered the underground chamber after the duke. He threw his hat across the small room and landed it on his bed.

His sister eyed him with something akin to growing suspicion.

"A rare kick-up? You mean you've been having fun?"

"Aye," said Chauncy, evidently pleased with himself as he followed his master into the room.

"What of Elly Bonner—and Hawkins?" asked his sister incredulously.

"Oh, Elly. No one saw her, but never mind that, Mand . . . wait till you hear what a capital time we've had."

"Capital time?" seethed Mandy. "Here I've been worrying my foolish head over you. I even went out to Witch's Elbow alone after . . ."

"Witch's Elbow?" ejaculated her brother, much struck. "Why the blister would you do that?"

"I was taking the shortcut to York, you horrid thing! Now what do you mean staying out so late and then having nothing more to say, but that you had a rare kick-up!"

"Indeed, Mandy," put in the duke with a grin, "it seems both Ned and Chauncy have won a bundle tonight." He had already received the particulars above-stairs.

"What? shrieked Mandy, not one bit mollified by this announcement. "Do you mean to tell me they've been out gambling?" She could see from the idiotic expression on her brother's face that that was precisely what they had been doing. She rose in fury, found his hat, and proceeded to beat him with it. She did this with some force, and he very naturally took precautions to protect himself by lowering his head behind his raised shoulder and arm, calling out protests all the while.

The duke put out a hand and captured Mandy's arm, firmly but gently calling a halt to her savagery.

"Heigh-ho, gamine! Let the lad explain."

"He has been gambling—and you want him to explain?"

"I rather think he should—don't you?" bantered the duke.

Ned agreed with the duke's logic and eyed his sister warily as he sat down on his bed. Chauncy grinned throughout the proceedings but offered not a word.

"Well then—do explain," said Mandy sweetly, shooting sparks all the while.

"Would have . . . if I'd been given a chance!" retorted her brother. However, he recalled the fat roll of ready in his pocket, and it rather sugared his temper. "Lordy, Mandy, never saw one before, you know. Heard of 'em . . . but not been to any of 'em. Grandfather always insisted they were for cits and laborers though I half suspect he attended a few in his heyday. It was famous good sport, and so I would have told him had he been around—miss him, you know," said he in way of accounting.

Mandy softened at once. "Oh, Neddy, so do I. But don't change the subject, m'buck. Explain yourself. What in faith are you talking about?"

"The Rat Pit, m'girl. Course you wouldn't know about it . . . don't think you'd like it—not that you're missish, can't say you are. Didn't think I'd like it either. But bang-up fun it was . . . and won us a roll of the ready!"

"Rat Pit?" questioned his sister doubtfully.

"I think your brother refers to a rather questionable sport, wherein they set a dog loose in a pit some six feet in diameter with an assortment of rats. He is expected to kill any number of these within a given space of time. It is on this particular point that bets are placed and money exchanged," explained the duke helpfully.

"Oh, Ned," said his sister with some disgust, "that is horrid!"

"Yes, it was, but Lordy, Mandy, it turned out to be . . ."

"I know—bang-up good fun!" said his sister, finishing the sentence for him contemptuously.

"Well . . . yes, it was," rejoined her brother, his smile fading as he considered the matter. "After all, the dog was not hurt—at least, not very much—and got rid of the ugly little brutes, you know. Good thing—too many rats about!"

"Neddy! That is the most bloodthirsty . . . odious thing. To bet money on some poor dog's ability to destroy . . ."

"Now, really, Mandy . . . coming on too strong, ain't you?" admonished her brother. "You aren't going to say 'poor rats'?"

She looked up and found the duke's amused eyes looking at her and giggled. It was not long before they all laughed—and Elly Bonner nearly forgotten. Yet the lady of their quest was not far away. In an abandoned quarry some four miles north of York, she sat at that very minute, and beside her was Jack Hawkins.

Elly Bonner was a tall thin girl, with a neat figure. Her light brown curls were pulled back into a bun. Her face was bright, with a well-scrubbed look.

The man sitting across the small table from her was a huge creature, well above average height. His dark hair curled round his heavy face. His eyes were dark and hard with distrust. He wore a peasant's shirt and loose trousers. He stared at the woman he had taken to his heart and considered his attachment. She was a good woman, was his Elly. Lord knew he didn't deserve her, but he had every intention of keeping her, no matter what the guv' said. He would have a job of it, though, and they'd have to move soon, for there was no talking her out of that book and the guv' was after her hide for it. He reached out across the table and took Elly's worn, rough-skinned hand in his own, patting it reassuringly. "Lookee' ere, lovey. Jest give it over to 'im, and we won't 'ave to worrit our 'eads over the cull no more!"

"I can't, Jack. I just can't. When we sail, we must send this book to the authorities. Lord Sherborne mustn't be allowed to hang for a crime he did not commit!"

"But if ye send that blasted book in, they'll catch guv! and . . ."

" . . . *and he is the murderer!*" she said uncompromisingly.

Jack Hawkins cast his eyes downward, not in shame but from fear of losing her. "So . . . am I."

She jumped up and went to him, putting her long, thin arms about his heavy shoulders. "No, Jack, you've fought. And yes, I know, you have killed a man in your time. But never a woman . . . and never in cold blood. You've fought your way through this life . . . God knows you've had to. But that cull . . . oh, he has killed in cold blood! And why? To keep poor Miss Celia from . . ."

"Hush now! Ye'll be blastin' me wit ye tears, and I won't 'ave it, Elly. Don't like to see ye cry. But Elly . . . it worrits me, it does. He been after me to tell him where we set up our ken. I won't. But he be a downy one—no tellin' when he'll find our lay. Got to get ye out. He won't let ye live, knowin' what ye know. . . ."

"Oh, Jack! We'll go away . . . we must. I want to

sail for the United States. 'Tis a grand land there—
where people like us can start a new life fresh and
clean, with the stink of the past well put behind! Please,
Jack, let's forget about the money and go to Bristol.
We can get a ship. I know we can."

" 'ow, Elly, girl? Jest tell me 'ow the bloody way we
can? Can't get passage without the blunt slapped down
on the table, and I can't make enough ridin' the high
toby—which ye don't take to anyways. Got to wait till
he heaves over m'fair share—and he best do that soon!"

"Oh, stop, Jack! You have to stop thinking like
a . . . thief!"

"Lordy, Elly, I been tryin'—for ye—I swear I
have. But you can't make a silk purse from a sow's
lug—ye jest can't!"

She sighed and patted his head, for she loved him.
She didn't know why, nor did she give a fig what he
had been. She only knew that she could make him so
much better and that she would. One day soon they
would make a home together . . . in the bright New
World across the ocean. They would have a roof over
their heads, children to laugh with . . . and food in
their bellies! Lord . . . they would . . . for it wasn't
too much to ask of life. . . .

Chapter Fifteen

Mandy was awakened the next morning by the rough shaking of her brother's hand. "Mandy, Mandy," he cried frantically. "We're done up, I tell you. Come on, we have got to get out of here. Chaunce is saddling our horses right this very minute!"

She rubbed her eyes in disbelief and frowned. "Oh, Neddy, let me sleep . . . do. . . ." she answered plaintively.

"Don't you understand, Mandy? *We have to leave!*" said her brother desperately.

"But why? I don't understand . . . what has happened?" she asked, suddenly aware that this was not one of her brother's larks.

"Chaunce and I went to the stream to get some fish for breakfast, and on the way back we saw Cook coming down the road on our old cob. Chaunce hailed her and wheedled a loaf of bread she had and was taking to her sister's, when we looked up and spotted Uncle coming down the road!"

"Good God!" ejaculated his sister.

"Just so, Mand. He tried to make as though he hadn't seen us. But he turned his horse right around and headed for Harrowgate. He is after the yeomen and back to fetch us. I just know it, for he saw clearly we were without horses. Even a dunce would put it together we are hiding in the ruins!"

"Lord, yes! Very well, nothing for it but to move." She dressed hurriedly and, without bothering to brush her tangle of curls, plopped a hat on her head. Scooping up the blankets, she rushed up the stone steps to the men above.

Quickly they were on their horses and crossing the glen for the viscount's woods, where they would make for the Old Track, when they heard the sound of horses' heavy hooves and knew themselves closely trailed.

"Nothing for it, Neddy, let's spring 'em!" cried Mandy, urging her horse into a gallop. It was a treacherous path through the woods, and many times they had to slow as the narrow route curved too sharply and met with broken branches. Then suddenly they heard the report of a gun, and Chauncy called to them to halt. They did, and Mandy frowned at her groom.

"Chaunce, they will be upon us."

"They seem to be armed, missy, and not above shooting at us. I don't give a fig for m'self, but it won't do to have either you or His Lordship winged!"

Ned sighed but held his head high. "He is quite right, Mandy. Don't worry. We shall stand buff."

"No!" screeched Mandy. "We shall run . . . we can outdo their paces . . . please, Neddy."

"No! It is not for a Sherborne to run and have his sister shot at. What sort of scoundrel do you take me for?"

She had no patience with this logic but knew it stemmed from a gentleman's strict code of honor! There was nothing for it but to wait her Uncle's onslaught! It came—such things inevitably do.

Squire Speenham, his breath coming in short spurts, his old-fashioned hat askew on his balding head, brought his horse to a halt before them, signaling the two yeomen to bring up the assembled party's rear.

Mandy noted the guns leveled at their heads and blushed hotly.

"Uncle Bevis—tell these men to put down their arms at once!"

"How dare you address me as Uncle, young lady! Dressed as you are . . . in the company of outlaws . . . for that is exactly what young Sherborne has become!"

"Oh, for the love of God!" said Ned with some exasperation, "stop your prattling, and do whatever it is you have to do!"

"And so I shall—though it grieves me deeply, much as you may suspect otherwise. My name is shamed." He turned to the older yeoman, his voice a command. "Take these gentlemen into Harrowgate with the least commotion you can. And see to it that their cell is well guarded.

They are to have *no* visitors!" He turned to his niece. "*You*, young woman, shall come with me!"

"No, I won't! I prefer the same fate as my brother," said Mandy defiantly.

"It perhaps will not surprise you to learn that I believe you may well deserve it. However, you are a gently bred female, though, at the moment, even that is held in doubt. You will return to my home and remain under constant supervision until your brother is brought to trial! Now come along!"

Neddy reached out a hand to comfort his sister and the younger yeoman, nervous in the sudden importance of his position, became overzealous. He brought down the gun hard on Ned's forearm, nearly dislocating him from his saddle. Lord Sherborne cried out with as much surprise as pain and turned a wrathful glance upon the yeoman.

Mandy screeched at the lad, "You dunce! I'll have your neck for that!"

"You'll not have anyone's neck! What sort of speech is that for a woman? It's not a moment too soon that I am taking you under hand!" thundered her outraged uncle. He turned back to the yeomen, "I'll have no rough manhandling from you two dolts! Lord Sherborne has not been convicted of any crime, though he must certainly be present to face the charges against him. His groom has done no more than any faithful servant. You will,treat them with respect. Now off with you, and as I said, *respect*—but with both eyes wide open!"

She sat her horse beside her uncle and watched as the yeomen took the reins of her brother and his groom. A low depression fell over her. Oddly enough, she thought of the duke and wished that he were here now. *Oh, faith, Brock . . . how we need you right now!*

"Shall we proceed, Amanda," said her uncle in a tight voice. His niece and nephew had put him to a great deal of embarrassment. Some had said that he had arranged for Ned's escape, and he had no liking for such talk. This would obviously put the tattlemongers in their place. After all, the Sherbornes were not blood relatives, their sins should not be visited upon his name in spite of the connection though, truth to tell, he would rather the entire mess had not occurred.

They said nothing all the way to the squire's mellow Tudor home. She was given over to the care of a parlor maid and taken to a guest room abovestairs. She was told a hot bath would be prepared for her, and then she heard a key turn in her door lock. There was nothing for it. She sank upon the blue coverlet of the brass bed and gave over to a fit of despondent tears.

At about this time, Chauncy and Ned were being led down the main pike to Harrowgate. On two occasions they had been told not to speak to one another, and thus no plan could be agreed upon. Chauncy suddenly winked at His Lordship and said quite loudly, "Och . . . Lordy, Lordy, lads but slow it up a mite . . ."

The yeomen exchanged glances as they turned in their saddles and considered the groom's choice of words. "What think ye is wrong with the bloke?"

The younger man shrugged his shoulders. "Nary a thing. Very likee he be trying to bamboozle us."

"Och, och . . . tis m'ole 'eart, it is. Canna ye stop a bit? There lads . . . look at me. I'm an old man . . and not up to all the gallivanting ye've put me through . . . oh . . . oh . . ."

It worked, the yeomen slowed their gait and just in time, it would appear, for Chauncy put a hand to his chest and discovered that his heart was no longer beating, and so he said, just before he fell off his horse, face down into the dirt road.

"Oh, bless the saints!" cried one of the yeoman jumping off his saddle, "we're in fer it we are. Likee they'll be blaming us for misusing the old codger!"

Ned jumped off his horse, and the younger yeoman then followed—lest he try to escape—and kept closer than was wise, for at that particular moment Chauncy made a most sudden recovery. Just as the short, wiry yeoman bent over him, he brought up his heavy fist and landed the hapless fellow a blow that sent him sprawling backward. Ned lost no time and took this opportunity to wrestle the gun away from the young yeoman at his side. 'Twas done, and both yeoman, conscious of their loss, blushing for their pride, lay tethered in the thick of the woods with their horses.

Ned and Chauncy were once more on their mounts, free to choose their way and heading northwest for Wharfe River. Ned very naturally felt a sense of exhilaration and exhibited his spirits by setting up a howl. Chauncy laughed and remembered the young lord's boyhood.

"Well now, laddie, we'll make for the river. We're bound to find a niche that will have to do. Won't be as cozy as has been, but, never mind that, missy ain't with us, so it don't much matter."

Ned frowned suddenly. "What of Mandy? What will Uncle do to her, Chaunce?"

"Lord love ye, nuthin a-tall! Don't you know? 'Twouldn't look well for him to go turning in his female kin. Miss Mandy be too well liked in these parts, and people would be bound to take her side of it. No, he'll keep her up at his ken a spell."

"She won't like that at all, Chaunce! I daresay she would rather be in prison."

"Bless ye, lad! She won't be there long. The duke be with us, ye know . . . and I fancy he won't take to the notion."

"That's right!" said Ned cheering up, "we have the duke!"

Time, a hot bath, and serious thinking had done wonders for Mandy's spirits. She brushed her hair until the gold shone like bright firelight. It was gathered atop her head, and the natural curls were allowed to cascade about her well-shaped face. Her dark eyes, though grave, were full with the determination that lighted sparks in their depths.

Some of her clothes had been brought from Sherborne Halls, and she had chosen a day gown of merry yellow muslin. It was of simple lines, yet it set off her alluring figure most attractively. She deliberately set the expression on her piquant face and wrinkled her nose as a knock sounded. She called out sardonically, "As the key is on the hall side of my door, you are free to enter as you wish, are you not?"

A maid of middle age and sour disposition put in her face.

"Sorry, miss. But Mr. Speenham wants you in the parlor for tea."

"Does he though?" said Mandy sweetly, defiance edging her words. "Tell Mr. Speenham that I have no wish for tea—or his company."

The maid cast her a superior glance. "He said you might take such a thing out of temper, but told me I

wasn't to return without ye, miss. So sorry to disoblige
. . . but Mr. Speenham says . . ."

"Oh, for goodness' sake! Very well," said Mandy,
walking past the maid and making for the stairs.

Amanda entered the neat parlor and brought her
dark eyes to Mr. Speenham's repulsive expression with
something akin to loathing. "Alfred! What an *un*pleasant surprise!" said she coming forward and taking up a
Windsor chair.

"Mandy! You are looking prodigiously well after
your . . . escapade," congratulated Mr. Speenham,
evidently determined to get on well with his house guest.

"Thank you, perhaps you should try a bit of the
same."

He frowned at her.

"You are coming it a bit too strong . . . why all
this hostility?"

"Because your father has seen to Ned's capture.
Don't you understand? We were trying to find Elly
Bonner, and how can we with Ned in a cell? How can
the both of you take such steps against your own relations? I find you both despicable in the extreme!"

"You shock me! Father and I want nothing but what
is right for both of you!" said Alfred, putting a hand to
his pale blue coat and brushing at some speck. "Really,
Amanda . . . I must say I never expected such things
from you."

She smiled sweetly at him and, had he a better understanding of her nature, he would have been prepared for
the sharp sting of her reply. "No, Alfred, of course, *you*
would not expect me to help my own brother. Being the
low creature you are . . . such things would never
cross your mind!"

He brought his brows together sharply.

"You are not in a position to criticize, are you?" his tone taunted.

She was frustrated and lashed out accordingly.

"When I am in your company sir, I have always that wondrous position!"

He stepped forward and took her by the shoulders. He wanted to slap her face but settled for a severe shaking.

"You are nought but a cockatrice . . . you brazen . . . I swear, you will live to rue your behavior towards me!"

He never knew what blasted him from his position. He only knew that a sudden force had managed to lift him bodily and fling him across the room. He landed against a Queen Anne chair, fell off balance, and dropped thuddingly to the Oriental carpet.

Mandy knew only that the violent handling of her person had ceased, that the source of this miracle had accomplished this without losing his breath, and that his glorious blue eyes were now caressing her face. "Are you quite all right, Mandy?" asked the duke gently, his voice low, soothing.

She nodded, unable to trust herself to verbal communication. He touched her cheek.

"Ned and Chauncy were not taken in. 'Tis all over Harrowgate. I met your uncle there. Rest assured, Chaunce will see them well hidden and safe . . . and so, my gamine, will you be." He took her hand and brought her to her feet, "Come."

At that particular moment, the butler arrived on the scene and announced, "Sir Owen Turndale," whereupon that gentleman entered and took in the spectacle of Alfred Speenham setting himself to rights and Amanda

Sherborne protectively ensconced in her guardian's powerful arm.

The scene displeased him, but he managed a grin.

"Well! It's amazing just how much can happen in the country!"

"Sir Owen," said Mandy, "you . . . were you in York . . . did you find Elly?"

"No, I am afraid not. However, I did learn that someone close to her, some fellow named Hawkins—it's the oddest thing—well, never mind that . . . ."

"What is the oddest thing?" queried the duke suddenly, his blue eyes intent upon Sir Owen's face.

"Just a thought, but never mind . . . 'twas but a slip of the tongue. This fellow Hawkins came in for supplies . . ." He was still frowning.

Alfred Speenham managed to recover enough to show some interest.

"What the deuce do we care about some fellow named Hawkins?"

"We don't," said Sir Owen, "except that he may lead us to Elly."

"And you say he was in York . . . buying supplies?" pursued Alfred.

"Yes, but what's this I hear of Ned and Chaunce? Did your uncle really try to take them in?" asked Sir Owen giving Mandy his full sympathy.

"Indeed he did. And he wants to keep me here under his supervision," said Mandy with a sigh.

"He shan't, gamine." said the duke. "Come . . . we should be going.

"Now hold on here," said Alfred Speenham, stepping forward, then checking himself as he remembered his earlier fate.

"Why?" said the duke eying him down.

"You just can't walk out of here with my cousin! My father is her uncle . . . and he is magistrate of this district . . . though he has chosen to overlook her crime. . . . "

"Speak like that, and I will take great pleasure in knocking out each and every tooth you possess in that sordid button mouth of yours!" threatened the duke. "You will remember that Miss Sherborne is *my* ward, not your father's. Further, until he chooses (though I recommend he think twice before taking such action) to bring charges against her, she need not take any advice, or commands from his direction!"

Sir Owen, his hands folded in his arms was standing slightly back, leaning against a near-by bookcase, and taking all this in with some interest. He did not like this, not any of it!

Alfred Speenham spluttered, his pride smashed, but he could find no answer. Mandy had an idiotic urge to stick her tongue out at him, but refrained from so unladylike a gesture and demurely followed her guardian to the door and out of the house.

Once upon horse and trotting down the drive, she gave way to a hoot.

"You were a hero! A great gun! A top sawyer! I do most humbly thank you!"

He laughed.

"It is absurd, but to hear you compliment me instead of insult me is more than I can bear. Do stop!"

She giggled and then turned sad eyes to him.

"You are certain Ned and Chaunce are safe?"

He laughed and regaled her with the tale he had heard of their daring escape, ending with, "It was all over Harrowgate. Your uncle was in a fit . . . almost foaming at the mouth!"

"But . . . where do you think they will go? How shall we find them?"

"For the moment, my gamine, we will not. And after all, there is no great need. Rely on Chaunce, Mandy. He will see them safely lodged, and he will get us word."

"Get us word? My goodness! How? Where are we going?" asked Mandy suddenly.

"Where do you want to go?" he asked quietly, "I can, of course, take you to Sherborne Halls—but I would then have to ask your aunt to vacate the premises for I won't have you under the same roof with that woman!"

"Do you think her involved then—in Celia's . . . murder?" asked Mandy on a whisper.

"No, but I don't think her a nice person. I have reasons for wanting her to remain where she is for now, Mandy. Therefore, I hope you will elect to come with me."

"With you? Where to?"

"To Skippy's manor," he said gently.

"Oh, no . . . I couldn't. I just could not."

"Nonsense. Forget what you heard last night. Eavesdropping is the eighth deadly sin," he said, his eyes twinkling.

"But . . . but . . . "

"Really gamine, you will find that Skip's . . . intrigues have nought to do with our own." He was laughing at her, she sensed, but somehow felt warmed by it, rather than angry.

"Very well . . . if you think so." She had no idea why she suddenly felt so complacent, so willing to rely on him. She only knew that it was a most comfortable sensation.

"Do you not think—under the unusual circumstances of our acquaintance—that you might find it more pleasing to call me Brock?"

She blushed. "No," she answered simply.

"I see," he said quietly, accepting this setback with grace. He proceeded to lift the heavy tenseness that had suddenly descended with a light easy chatter, exerting all the charm that had made him one of London's most delightful rakehells!

Chapter Sixteen

Elly Bonner sat rigid with fright as she stared at the boxes her Jack was piling upon their cavern table. She knew now where he had been and what he had been doing. Half of her wanted to scold, and half of her longed to go through the treasures he was setting before her!

"Faith! I declare, Jack. What's this ye be bringing down around m'poor head?"

"Jest wait, Elly . . . 'tis fit fer the Queen ye be!" exclaimed her man, merry as a boy.

"Oh, Jack . . . so many things . . . how? We done spent the last of our ready more'n a week ago."

"Aw, now, Elly girl . . . don't take on like a shrew! 'Tis fer ye . . . all of it . . . fer ye. Ready-made they be, but I swear, one day ye'll be wearing those that ain't!"

"Oh, Jack!" He was like a child pleased as punch that he walked for the first time. The fact that he had walked into a field of poison ivy was irrelevant at that marvelous moment. She persisted.

"How, Jack, how?"

"Aw, go on, Elly . . . don't be pushin' me a basket full of silly questions. Open 'em," he said, throwing off the cover of the first large white box. His large burly hands produced a pretty muslin day dress of blue print, and he beamed at her as he swayed it through the air.

She gasped, and her hand trembled as it reached out to touch the soft alluring material, so much in contrast with the brown drab she wore. "Oh, Jack, m'own darlin' Jack, 'tis grand! Oh, that grand . . . but . . . "

"And this, Elly girl!" he interpolated, throwing off another lid and producing a yellow straw bonnet with a pale blue ribbon. "And Lordy, I got ye half boots of brown kid . . . and these blue slippers. . . ." He dove into his packages and produced the footwear, shoving them at her in his frenzy. ". . . and a cloak . . ." He made to find it, but she halted him with her touch. They stared into one another's eyes, and she fell into his huge embrace and cried. He stroked her head and wondered at the depth of emotion she could evoke from him—him, who had never blinked when he rode the high toby and took sparklers off the flash coves and noble ladies. Him, who'd thrashed his own father when he had had enough—him, who had killed a man in his fury for no more reason than being called a fool. He had beat him, stabbed him—and yet here he was near to tears for the love of a woman. 'Twas a queer thing, he told himself, and pushed her gently away.

"Tomorrow, I'll be gettin' us a cob and gig, and we'll head for Bristol, m'girl. We'll get a ship . . . the first one headin' for that new land of yers . . . "

"But Jack, Jack . . . where did ye get the money?" She pleaded for an answer, already knowing it.

"Aw now, Elly . . . "

"Jack!" she insisted.

He sighed, she'd have her way, she was like that. "Bless ye, girl . . . I took it! 'Twas not even a quarter of m'fair share!"

She gasped.

"You . . . you went to the waterfall . . . you took the gold! Oh, my God! Never say you spent it."

"Lordy girl, they didn't give me these things coz of m'fine face!" he sneered gruffly.

"But Jack . . . he was right about that. He told you it couldn't be spent yet. 'Tis newly minted sovereigns . . . they haven't been in circulation in the North long enough . . . Jack, they'll trace it to ye."

"No, they won't, coz I won't be here. We'll be leaving come the end of this week. Didn't I tell ye? I told the livery to have m'gig and a horse—jest a cob, seein' as we'll be leavin' him at Bristol."

"But . . . oh, Jack, if he finds out . . . ?"

"He won't! I made the chest look untouched, I did. I ain't so dimwitted as some might think."

"Of course, you're not!" she reassured him. "But . . . "

"No more of it will I take . . . we be going to get

ye that dream of yers, jest like I promised!" He grinned, truly pleased with himself. "Now come, Elly girl. Come see what else I got 'ere!"

She consented, for she loved him, and there was no sense arguing. Besides, the boxes held too much magic, they were too great a temptation. It was not long before the two were dancing about their wares like children at a festival.

The duke saw Mandy to the viscount's house, and set about in his authoritative manner to have things readied for her stay. A lackey was despatched to Sherborne Halls to collect some of the clothes she would need. A parlor maid was sent scurrying up the stairs to ready the yellow guest room, and the butler ordered a footman to advise the viscount (who was again closeted with his man of business) to come as soon as he could to the library, where he was wanted by his noble guest.

His Grace then turned quizzical eyes on his ward and suggested that she might wish to be taken to her room for a short rest before dinner.

She frowned at him. He was in her good graces, therefore she was well disposed to please him and obey any reasonable request. This, however did not constitute anything resembling what she thought was reasonable. "You are trying to be rid of me. Why?"

He flicked her nose and chuckled, bringing a flood of warmth to her fair cheeks.

"Because, my ward, I think that I should have some time alone with Skippy before you make your appearance. He will be most shocked at all that has occurred, because he knows nothing of what has passed this day.

I think it best that he learn it from me, before I blast him with what you overheard last night."

"What?" she shrieked. "Never say you are going to tell him?"

"Most certainly. I think he deserves to know what you overheard and to be given the opportunity to explain, if he deems fit."

"Then I should be here to hear what he has to say," she countered.

"No. This is not for a female."

"That is most odious of you!" she snapped.

"Ah, how much better I feel now," he bantered. "We are back to our former standards."

She pouted and turned in a huff, but his voice brought her head back, "Mandy?"

"Yes, Your Grace."

He knew not what he wanted to say.

"Rest well!"

She took this as a taunt and put up her chin before making for the stairs, leaving him to watch her go. The duke smiled to himself as he observed her hurried skip up the horseshoe-shaped staircase. He was not aware that his smile caressed her form, only that a glowing sensation was spreading throughout his body at the thought of having her here under his protection. He sighed happily and turned to cross the marble flooring to the library doors.

He had not long to wait, for he had scarcely poured the brandy into his glass before the viscount descended upon him.

"Brock! Thank God, you've come to interrupt me! Another moment with that dratted dolt, and I'd have been near to pulling m'hair out! Lord! He is a damn good agent, but the devil of a proser!" He spied the brandy and added, "Pour me one while you're at it."

The duke grinned and handed him a glass, taking up a chair opposite his friend who stretched himself lengthwise on the sofa, heedless of the elegant yellow brocade.

"Have a roll of news for you, Skip," said the duke idly.

"Eh? What is it?"

"The twins. I'll give it to you quickly. It seems Ned and Chauncy—as well as Amanda—were chased by their uncle and two yeomen. When fired upon . . ."

"Good God! Upon my soul, never say that devil Bevis allowed his own kin to be shot at?"

"He did, though the shots may have been in the air. However, Ned would not run with his sister in danger."

"Excellent lad! Always knew he was a right . . ."

"Shall I continue?" said the duke sweetly.

"Indeed, do!"

He then proceeded to inform his friend of all the lurid details, ending with the statement that Mandy was now safely tucked in abovestairs.

"By Jupiter! What an adventure you are all having! Ah, well!" sighed the viscount sadly.

"It would seem that *you* are having a little adventure of your own, Skip," said the duke meaningfully.

"Eh? What's that you're driving at?"

"I am certainly not interested in names, so I'll not ask for them, but Mandy was out in the woods last night—your woods—about midnight . . ."

"Good God!" exclaimed the viscount, sitting bolt upright, "Never say . . ."

"I am afraid so, Skip. But worse than that, it gives credence to what Sir Owen has been hinting at."

Skippy ran his hands through his sandy hair. "Demme, but I'm in a tangle, Brock. Very well—I know I can trust you, so I will, but 'tis to go no further!"

The duke nodded his head in assent to this, and the viscount began with his tale. "It was just after I had discovered Celia was . . . shall we say . . . not the sort I wanted for wife, that I met Kathline. It was at an assembly in Harrowgate. She is Irish, and she and her father were on holiday at his sister's, when her father had some sort of heart attack. The doctor pronounced him dangerously ill. He can't sustain any shocks, you see . . . he can't be moved because he is dying.

"We fell in love, but you already must be aware of that. At any rate, her father forbade the match. She is Catholic, and he wouldn't hear of her taking an English Protestant husband. We continued to meet, and two months ago she became of age. I obtained a special license, and we were married in secret."

"Blister it!" exclaimed the duke. "You did what?"

"I married her. Yet we cannot announce it for fear it would kill her father. She can't have that on her conscience, you see. Her aunt knows of our marriage and helps us to keep it from him, but Kathline wants him to die in peace. The doctor says it will be soon."

"Good Lord, Skip, I suppose I should felicitate you. Though in truth . . . "

"You should, for she is everything to me," said the viscount, suddenly going off into another world.

"Very well then, man, I do! And I suppose this explains all your strange behavior," rallied the duke.

The viscount colored. "But Brock, you must see—it does rather give me a motive."

"For murder?"

"Indeed, Brock. They could have it that she—Celia —was carrying my child and tried to blackmail me when she discovered I was already married. After all, it would be natural for a husband to want such a thing kept from his wife. And in my case, I have the added necessity of keeping my marriage a secret!"

"So you think you look a bit havey-cavey? Very well, agreed—to anyone who did not know you, it might look smoky. But Skip, *you* ain't been accused!" shot the duke, grinning.

"By Jove! That's right, ain't it? But that damnable fellow means to have a case against me . . . to spare Ned and pave the way to Amanda."

"Sir Owen, you mean?"

"Certainly, Sir Owen. Trouble-making gamster . . . after Mandy, mark me!"

"Yes, after Mandy. And much in need of money. Which brings us clear across to something else we must discuss."

"Eh?"

"I met with Fowler and we discussed some very interesting possibilities. By the way, you know he is a runner, but he is not here on account of Ned Sherborne."

"Upon my soul! What then?

"Gold, m'bucko—three chests of the new sovereigns!" replied the duke smiling at his friend's astonishment.

"So, that's why you went flying out of here the

other day," said the viscount more to himself than to the duke. "What gold?"

"A shipment of the new coins was scheduled to leave Barings Bank in York for Barings in Manchester to cover the paper currency that had been collected. A leak worked its way to Mrs. Brinley . . . and I imagine, through her to Celia. One can only speculate who then received the information. At any rate, the coach must have been waylaid, for its drivers and two guards have vanished!"

"Poor fellows! Killed, you think?"

"Undoubtedly, old boy, what else? Their families have not a word from them," the duke answered grimly.

"You think you know, don't you?" asked Skippy, his eyes narrowing as he caught the look on the duke's face.

"I may—for there are really only two possibilities," said the duke. "Whom do you know in desperate need of money?"

"By Jove!" said Skippy. "Never say you think it is . . ."

Chapter Seventeen

The guv', as Jack Hawkins had learned to refer to the mastermind of the gold theft, was at that particular moment engaged in a hardline conversation in York. There were debts, gaming debts, he had accumulated and they were up for demand. A gentleman of honor discharged these debts before all others, for the code was *play and pay!*

Marriage to Amanda Sherborne was a desperate need, for his lifestyle was wont to be costly, but that mariage, should it ever take place, would not attend to his pressing debts. He had in the end gone to a moneylender. Now, his first interest payment was due. He needed another month—just one more month for the gold to go into circulation, but he could not very well explain this to the small, bearded man sitting before him. Another story was concocted, and his diamond stick pin and gold watch left in lieu of payment before he was able to depart.

Soon afterward as he was crossing the cobbled street toward the livery stables, he saw a small gathering of people. Curious, he sidled near and heard a store owner saying for the benefit of his audience, "Bless me, Mr. Fowler, it weren't my fault! Didn't notice that the mint was different until he left the store. But I won't hand it in . . . 'tis mine, coz he walked off with m'wares, he did!"

"But the gold is not in circulation yet, and it has been identified as stolen from Barings Bank," argued Mr. Fowler.

Guv's brow went up expressively, and he departed the scene. He pulled a face, thinking ruefully that the fool Jack Hawkins had gone too far! He had been trying to get Jack to tell him where he was holed up with Elly Bonner, but the man had gone so far as to threaten him away. He wanted that diary and so he had told Jack, but Hawkins was a stubborn creature, saying only that his Elly had it safe and nobody was going to come nigh her.

He already knew that Jack had been to town to buy supplies and such, but he hadn't been aware that the dratted fool had used the gold. This could not be allowed.

It was still light out when Jack left the enclosed chamber of the quarry and saddled his horse. He had with him two burlap bags and a horsehair blanket. He cut through the Old Track and, heedless of Witch's

Elbow and its demons, he made his way through the moors, heading for Wharfe River. Some twenty-five minutes later, he was on foot and leading his mount along the river bank, up a steep incline until a waterfall some ten feet in width and hundred feet in height came into sight and sound. Its foaming cascade fell into the semienclosed pool at its base before the river current met and swept away what it had to offer.

Here, Jack tethered his horse behind some evergreens and climbed down over the boulders to a niche beside the falls. An observer would have been astounded, for at that moment he vanished.

Actually, he had slipped behind the waterfall to a limestone crevice which extended back some fifty yards under the river and behind the falls, narrowing to a point where only the very thinnest of men could slide through. It housed along its damp dark walls three wooden boxes trimmed with metal and bearing some kind of official seals.

Hawkins made his way to one of these and flung open the top, licking his lips as the coins glittered at him. They had killed those poor blokes for this, but that didn't matter—though, in truth, he didn't hold with killing that poor young guard. After all, he had thrown in his lot with them, and Hawkins believed in fair play. It had all happened so fast. They had held up the coach as planned; everything had gone so smoothly, and he watched guv' coldly put a bullet into the two drivers and the one remaining guard. It was not the original plan. He wondered at first if guv' would let them live after they had seen his phiz. He had made that young guard tie and gag them, and then he shot them, weighted them, and gave them to

the river. The coach received the same watery fate after
they had brought the gold into the cave. That took some
doing with all their combined strength. Then guv', he
had that look in his eye, and the young guard was
dead. 'Twas his fault—he kept crying about guv' killing
the others—kept saying he didn't agree to anything
like that.

Well, he wasn't sitting around waiting for guv' to
point his pistol in his direction. No, sir . . not Jack
Hawkins! He put his hands through the gold and smiled.
Him and Elly . . . this was going to buy a few
dreams.

"Well, well, Jack! Thought you might come here
again! A bit greedy, ain't you?" sneered a figure standing in the arched opening of the cave. "I should have
realized you didn't have the sense to wait it out. Didn't
really want to eliminate you. Thought we might do
business again in the future—one never knows!"

"Guv', let me explain," Jack began, for a pistol was
aimed at his head, and he had forgotten to bring his
own. He tried to get to his feet, but the man ordered
him down.

"On your knees, you dolt! First, Jack, if you mean
to retain that worthless life of yours, where is Elly
and the diary?"

"Go to the divil!"

"Jack! Just tell me that, and we'll forget about this
lapse of sense you've had."

"Elly be my woman. You ain't puttin' a hole in her
head the way you done the others."

"There is no need for that, provided you get me the
diary!" said the man softly.

"She won't give it up, and I ain't about to make her!" said Jack stubbornly.

"Then you are a dead man!" said the guv', his nostrils flaring with anger.

"You kill me, guv', and she'll be after yer hide," threatened Jack.

"Precisely so!" said the man, firing one deadly shot, putting an end to the big man's life with the touch of a finger. "Precisely so, Jack. She will come in search of you. And then I shall have her—and the diary!"

He left a dead man lying on the hard cold ground of the cave. He left, without feeling, without thinking beyond his own needs, the shattered body of a man, whose death would bring about the end of Elly Bonner's hopes. But what did he care for such things? He unsaddled Jack's horse and threw the worn leather into the river, not waiting to see it sink. He slapped the horse's flanks and watched it trot away, then mounted his own horse, for he was already late for dinner.

At the viscount's establishment dinner went quite well, with all three in high spirits. Mandy appeared fetching in her white muslin gown, her gold ringlets cascading about her pert face. She put a small chocolate cake to her mouth and took a bite and made an appreciative sound.

"Hmmm . . . poor Neddy . . . he does so love this sort of sweetcake."

The duke's eyes caressed her. "Ned will be eating them soon enough, gamine . . . don't fret."

The viscount observed this with all due astonishment and said nothing about it. His friend had flirted outrageously with every sort of beauty from the time he had first known him. It was not unusual for him to come on strong with any pretty female, though his intentions were lighthearted. However, he had never seen him play loose and fast with a maid, nor did he expect it of his friend in the position he held as guardian over Mandy. Yet, there he was . . . Egad! thought the viscount taking full note of the duke's expression, the dog is in love! He ain't flirting, he is drinking deep. Demme! Brock in love? And with a chit too high spirited to ever fall in with his libertine ways! Demme! But this is funny!

Skip attracted their attention by suddenly laughing quite loudly.

Two pairs of eyes turned his way, and the duke asked casually, "What's the joke, Skip?"

Skip looked up into the duke's blue eyes, found the question exquisitely humorous, and began to shake with mirth.

"Skip," objected Mandy, "what *is* so funny?"

The viscount tried to recoup his self-composure and measured off his laughter in spurts.

"Nothing . . . ain't suitable for a female," he attempted in way of explanation.

"Oh, well, then, you shall give the joke to me later —is that it?" asked the duke, putting up a brow, for somehow he knew 'twas a take-in.

"Oh . . . oh, of course, Brock," said the viscount, avoiding his friend's eyes.

"Well, I think you are both horrid! Why should it not be fit for my ears? My brother tells me more than you can imagine . . . and I promise you I would understand!"

The duke cast her an amused glance.

"No doubt you would, gamine, but you shouldn't!"

"Humph!" Mandy responded, rising. "I suppose, then, I should be leaving you to linger over your port —and your jests?"

The viscount jumped hastily to his feet. "What . . . and leave you all to yourself? What sort of poor host do you take me for, Mand . . ? Come on now, let's all retire to the library. 'Tis chilly enough tonight to have Sticwell have a fire lit for us."

Some fifteen miles northwest, in the heart of the Dales lay a tavern well hidden from the road. Its location was such that travelers never came its way, or when they did, one glance at the shabbiness of the building quickly set them back on the road again. It happened that Chaunce remembered a friend who frequented this particular inn, and it was there he led his young lord.

The tavern's large public galley was low ceilinged, its oak rafters and wall beams lined dirty, yellow-painted walls. Various nondescript paintings hung here and there, many of them tilted off balance. Its oak wood floors sloped with age, and its tables and chairs were crude with wear. However, its inhabitants minded none of these failings.

They swayed, boomed, and made merry with raucous good mirth, and in spite of the tavern's seclusion, its rooms were full. The tavern housed several unusual individuals whose occupations put them in need of such a retreat. They welcomed the seclusion and paid well for their lodgment. This particular inn maintained one room which they kept uninhabited. It was called the "Boiler." This was because of the legend connected with its use. Some hundred years ago, it was said the tavernkeeper and his wife would put up lonely travelers in this choice room. The bed had a trick spring which when pulled, lowered its occupant into a huge cast iron container filled with boiling water. The hapless traveler's money was kept by the evil pair. This prodigious sort of murder and theft went on for some time, until a vigilant young woman in search of her husband, discovered the mode of his disposal. Being of sound body, if not mind, the innkeeper's wife balked and was never heard of again, but her husband was hanged for his crimes, and the room was sealed.

The cast iron container, however, was still in position, and the room always ready, should a redbreast chance along to give the merry men of the tavern trouble they didn't want. So the present owner often assured his guests.

Chauncy and Ned had not been in the inn above five minutes, when Chauncy felt it prudent to regale the coterie with their day's adventure. Needless to say, this won them a place in these worthies' hearts, and it was ale all round, and soon wenches were attending their needs.

In fact, at the very moment Mandy felt her twinge of guilt for eating her brother's favorite cake, Ned was swinging a pretty barmaid on his knee. In his free hand he waved a tankard of foaming ale and thought himself well occupied.

Chaunce, not far behind in much of the same, had

sought privacy abovestairs with the pretty of his choice. Thus it was that both of Mandy's lifelong male companions were quite content.

Elly Bonner had no such solace. She stared at the walls of the quarry chamber and wrung her hands fretfully. She paced the room as though she were some caged animal, for never before had Jack stayed out all night. At first, she thought he'd gone to some tavern for a pint of ale. Then she worried that he'd found some wench to while away the hours. But not Jack . . . he was not that kind. He was a one-woman man, he was. She knew it—she just knew it. He wouldn't do that to her—to what they shared.

Morning came, though its light could not filter down into the blackness of her hideaway, yet she awoke with a start. Looking round her, she hoped and called, "Jack?"

The single candle had burned out. She lit another and called again, yet feeling all the while she was alone, "Jack?"

Then all at once she knew. She felt it, as though she could feel the essence of him fade before her. He was gone—but he couldn't be. She wouldn't let him be. She got to her feet and started pacing, fist to mouth. He said he was going to Pitman Bay, up the Wharfe River—to that waterfall cave he had told her about. Well, she would go there herself. Perhaps he was hurt, lying about waiting for help.

She washed quickly, fixing a mobcap on her hair, and settling a wool knit shawl about her shoulders. It was a ten-mile hike to Pitman Bay from her quarry, but somehow she would make it. She had to. Hugging the diary to herself, she began her journey.

She was overtaken by a farmer on the main pike and accepted a ride as far as Harrowgate, where she slipped off with a hurried smile and a gentle thank-you. She cut through the woods and, walking steadily, put the remaining six miles behind her. It was noon before she reached Pitman Bay and started traveling up the river, hugging its bank closely. She didn't know exactly where the falls was, but she would find it—had to find it. She remembered clearly his description of it, how he had explained the way of entering its hidden crevice. Then she heard the rumbling and rushing of water—thank God!

She clutched at the diary, lest it slip to the waters below, and began the climb over the boulders and rocks, scratching her legs, tearing her drab gown, and finally making it to the waterfall. It couldn't be seen, the opening Jack had spoken of. It appeared to be solid rock under that avalanche of white foam. She approached the corner lip and, pushing aside the bush, there behind the falls, she saw the huge, arched opening. She slipped in as though she were entering a new world. 'Twas frightening, and she had a foreboding of evil as she stood there looking into its dim chamber.

She saw the three chests of gold lined up against the wall and then, almost immediately, she saw Jack's slumped form. She knew the moment she saw him—even before she saw him she knew. Yet still she hoped and ran to him, calling his name. She dropped the diary and bent over his figure. His face was in the dirt and she turned him over, brushing the soil away from his cheeks. Her sorrow was her own, and she suffered in her own private way. She put her hands over her eyes to shield the sight of his blood, dried—cold, but the vision remained.

Then she thought of his murderer . . . and of her revenge . . . and of justice for Jack. She picked up the diary and put it in Jack's hands and covered him with her shawl. She would have to get help. But whom could she trust? The Sherbornes were not to be found —hiding from the law—because of him—that murdering swine—but then who?

She walked out of the cave for a lungful of fresh air. Then she remembered the Viscount Skippendon. An hour's walk brought her to the edge of his woods, and some twenty minutes later she was walking down the front drive to his house. She was exhausted and her heart nearly numb, but this was something she would see through.

Mandy was in the library, her legs tucked under her pink muslin gown. Her gold ringlets swirled about her pretty head as she dipped her shortcake biscuits into her hot tea. She was alone and quite bored with her day. Mr. Fowler had come to see the duke and had taken His Grace and the viscount off with him to visit with Mrs. Brinley. She wondered what a Bow Street runner had to do with her aunt. Mandy had to stay in her room, the duke said, while Fowler was there, for he didn't want the rascally fellow asking her any questions. She had deemed it only prudent to comply. No word had been brought to her about Ned and Chaunce, and by now she was in a fidget!

The sound of a heavy thud on the front door of the house brought her head up with interest. It was the only one she had heard all day, and she was curious. She waited, her ears pricked up like a kitten's. Sticwell's tone, though not his words, could be heard, and he seemed as though he were being rude to the party seeking admission. She went to the hall doors and looked out.

"Look here, young woman, the viscount is not in and, even if he were, you don't really think I would admit *you* to his presence?"

"Please," begged Elly. She knew her appearance was ragged and dusty, but somehow she had to get in and wait for the viscount. "Ye must allow me in . . . I will wait . . . anywhere ye deem fit . . . ye see, I have walked all the way from . . ."

"My God!" exploded Mandy, running forward. "Stand aside, Sticwell." She went to Elly and put a comforting arm about the woman's drooping shoulders, "Elly . . . you poor, poor dear." Mandy turned an angry eye on Sticwell for his pompousness. "You will see to it at once, sir, that a fresh pot of tea and biscuits are brought to the library for Miss Bonner!"

"Very good, miss," said Sticwell. Miss was an honored guest, and he dared not incur her displeasure further, though he felt it sacrilege to entertain such a woman in the library.

Mandy led Elly into that room and kicked the door shut behind her with the toe of her dainty pink slippers. She saw Elly comfortably seated on the sofa and then went to the sherry decanter and poured a rather large portion. Bringing it to the woman, she said firmly, "Drink this."

Elly did—in one gulp—and then closed her eyes. Mandy took the empty glass and put it on the table before dropping down beside her. As she waited for Elly to recover herself, she patted her work-worn hand. Finally, Elly opened her eyes and said,

"Oh, miss, 'tis that glad I am to see ye."

"Elly, where have you been all these weeks? We have been searching for you everywhere," said Mandy, now taking up a chair to face her.

"I been hiding in that old quarry no one's used in years. Jest a bit north of York. Me and m'man Jack." Tears formed in her eyes, causing them to glisten with pain. "He be dead . . . m'man . . . shot in the head . . . and his body . . . cold. . . ."

"My God! How! Who! Elly . . . explain," said Mandy, leaning over to touch the woman's hand again. However, the footman entered just then with the tea tray, and they waited for him to place this on the serving table between them and depart before speaking.

Mandy poured and pushed the cup of the hot dark brew toward Elly.

"Here . . . drink this . . . you must! You have had a terrible shock and will need all your wits and health to get you through it."

"Don't want to get through it! Oh, Lordy! Wish I was dead with m'Jack." She fell into her hands and gave over to weeping. Mandy went on her knees beside her and silently stroked the woman's bent head. She said nothing, but allowed Elly to relieve her pent-up grief. After a time, Elly pushed back her straying locks and sniffled. Again Mandy pressed the teacup at her, "Drink this . . . do, Elly."

She sat on the floor and watched the wretched

creature sip at the soothing drink before attempting to fathom what had happened.

"In the cave—the waterfall cave—with the gold," said Elly somewhat numbly.

"Gold . . . what gold?" asked Mandy, thoroughly perplexed.

"It don't matter . . . do it? He be dead . . . 'twas all for nought," Elly said bitterly.

"Elly, I don't understand. How did all this come about?" Mandy was trying to get at the heart of it.

"We wanted to get away. I swear I was goin' to send ye Miss Celia's diary . . . I swear it, Miss Amanda," said the woman pitifully.

"The diary? You mean you have the diary safe?" Mandy's voice was suddenly hopeful.

"Aye, I have it safe," said the woman numbly.

"But where, Elly, where?"

"It be with Jack—he be keepin' it fer me."

"But Elly," said Mandy gently. "You have said that Jack is . . ."

"I know . . . but he hold the book . . . gave it over to him, I did, and come here."

"And Jack is with this gold you speak of?" tried Mandy.

"Aye."

"Then can you take me there? I know you are weary, and I do promise you, Elly, as soon as we have the diary you shall rest. But you must see how important it is that we get the thing into someone's hands. My brother's life depends on it!"

"Aye—and Jack's soul. Come, Miss, I'll take ye there for ye'll never find it on yer own."

They rose and made their way out of the house. Mandy did not even bother to put a shawl about her shoulders, and she was too excited to feel that the wind had turned cold.

She ordered the stable boys to saddle her own horse and one of the viscount's for Elly. They cast the weary woman a doubtful look, but Amanda Sherborne was a guest (for all the scandal about her) in their employer's house, and they had no choice in the matter.

Some ten minutes later they were riding out into the gray light towards the river. Elly was not an experienced rider, and they had to take it slowly for the most part. Mandy cast sharp looks at the woman and felt her heart go out to her, for she was living in her own cell of quiet pain.

The duke rose from the table at the Cock Pit. "Well, Mr. Fowler, you have now in your possession enough facts to go and question the scoundrel."

"Aye, and make it first thing tomorrow, sir, for demme, he must be in a wild state over that Hawkins spending the gold. We know now it must be somewhere in the vicinity," said the viscount, also rising.

Mr. Fowler considered them. "That I will, gentlemen. But it be touchy . . . *he* ain't spent the gold, and we ain't got nuttin to put him and this 'ere Hawkins together."

"True, but we may yet trip them up," said the duke. "Good-day to you," he said, as he went outdoors with the viscount to order up their horses.

"Egad, Brock! You are in a sudden fidget to leave. Had in mind to partake another ale," complained Skippy, mounting his horse.

The duke frowned. "I don't know what it is, Skip, but I got this uncomfortable sensation that something ain't what it should be. Besides, leave Mandy to herself all day, and there is no telling what mischief she may get into. Think we had better ride." he said, sending his horse into a canter.

They made it home in less than twenty minutes and strode purposefully toward the house, the viscount making plaintive noises for the duke to slow down a bit.

"Zounds, old boy! She'll be there, see if she won't."

They were given entrance by Sticwell and, as they strode past him toward the library, the duke ordered lightly, "Have Miss Amanda join us in the library—if she has no objections."

Not waiting for an answer, they proceeded to the room and continued the lively discussion regarding racing horses which the viscount had introduced en route. The butler followed and stood at the threshold of the room, clearing his throat.

The viscount glanced up and said sharply, "Damme, Sticwell, if you've got something stuck in your track, go and drop some firewater in it! Don't stand about giving us a symphony!"

"I think . . ." said the duke drily, a twinkle in his eye, "that he is *trying* to tell us something."

"Oh, are you?" said the Viscount surprised. The butler nodded. "Well, then, Stic, go on. We won't bite your head off, you know!"

" 'Tis Miss Amanda," said Sticwell. "You asked me to have her called. But I am afraid she is not in."

"Not in?" said the duke rounding on him, "What do you mean? Where is she then?"

"I really couldn't say," said Sticwell, hoping the young woman, and not himself, would be the object of the duke's wrath.

"Can't say? Didn't she leave a message?" asked the duke.

"No, Your Grace, she did not leave any message. She simply ran out of here."

"Ran out, you say?" said the viscount, frowning. "Just like Mandy, forever running here or there . . . not at all a restful female."

"Ran out? By herself?" inquired the duke, narrowing his blue eyes and thinking the butler was being deliberately difficult.

"No, Your Grace. I tried to keep the female out, but Miss insisted on showing her in. And then they left—together."

"What female?" asked the viscount, "Damme, man, don't give it to us in bits and pieces! Speak up, speak up!"

"She said her name was Elly Bonner," said Sticwell, much surprised by the expression that passed between His Grace and the viscount.

"Dismissed, Sticwell," said the viscount. They waited for the man to depart before speaking.

"Elly Bonner came here? I don't like it," said the duke. "Something is wrong, I feel it, Skip!"

However, they were not given the opportunity to speculate fully, for the library doors then burst open, admittingly a lovely, tall female in an exquisitely designed white spencer over a white muslin gown. Her dark ringlets were held with white ribbons and her lips were parted with Skippy's name. "John," she cried and went directly into his arms, heedless of the duke's presence.

This name elicited yet another. "Kathy!"

The duke watched this scene, torn between impatience and amusement. He could do nothing but await its outcome. The viscount recalled the duke's overwhelming company and took a moment from gazing into his wife's eyes to introduce them.

"I have the honor, Brock, to present my wife, Kathline, to you." He turned to the woman, "This is the Duke of Margate, Brock Haydon, my dearest friend."

She was poised in her reply and gave the duke a fleeting smile, as he bent over her hand. "So pleased . . . yes, you must know that John has often said your name . . . with much fondness. Do excuse my strange . . . intrusion. I have received . . . something of a shock and am not myself."

"A shock?" asked Skippy, turning her in his arms. "Darling, what is it?"

She cast a doubtful glance at the duke, and he begged to be excused, but she stayed him. "Oh, no, sir, you needn't leave. It's just that . . . you see, my father's dead. . . ."

She fell onto her husband's chest and gave over to sobbing. The duke offered his condolences and then quietly let himself out of the room. In the hallway, he stood frowning, unsure what to do next. Mandy was gone . . . where?

It was at just about that moment the two women in question arrived at the waterfall cave. Mandy marveled that she and Ned had never come across it as children. She then remembered Elly's grief and silently rebuked herself as she entered the arched opening of the cave.

She watched as Elly walked straight to Jack and she winced to see the woman bend over the slumped figure and speak quietly to it as though he were still alive. The diary was produced, and Mandy went to it, just barely concealing her excitement. "Oh, Elly! Why did you keep it so long?"

"You see, miss, m'Jack . . . was mixed up in this." She went to one of the chests and threw open the lid.

Mandy gasped. "My God! That's what you meant by gold. But I still don't understand . . ."

Elly suddenly put her fingers to her lips. Then before Mandy knew what she was about, Elly grabbed the book from her hands and dived to Jack's body, burying it beneath his side. Mandy watched her openmouthed, thinking perhaps the shock the girl had sustained had been too much for her, until she followed Elly's eyes to the arched opening and discovered there a darkly clad figure obscuring what little light there was.

Mandy gasped until she realized the figure in the black cape was her cousin, Alfred Speenham, and then her tone took on its usual contempt for him.

"Oh Alfred, you gave us a fright. However did you find this cave . . . and what, in fact, brings you here?"

He smiled and there was something evil in his eyes.

"Then you still don't know, do you? I thought when I saw you riding this way with Elly you must already know. You are not so clever as you suppose, Amanda," and it was then he brought up his pistol.

"What do you mean? What is he talking about, Elly? What is it that I don't know yet?"

"Hush, miss. What you don't know . . . will keep you a bit longer, I'm thinking. . . ."

"Then you are thinking wrong, m'girl!" snapped Alfred. "I thought that when Jack didn't show up, you would come along, and I was right. So sorry, Amanda. Didn't mean for you to get caught up in this. Meant to marry you to please m'dad and keep what's mine. I'm afraid you two will have a swimming accident."

"Alfred . . . oh, my God! It was *you!*"

"Of course. It was always me Celia wanted. She wanted to be a lady and live comfortable, I wanted what she had to give. Then she learned from Aunt Agatha about the gold shipment, and when she heard of its theft, she thought to blackmail me into marrying her . . . or failing that, into paying her for her silence. I chose to do otherwise."

"But why? You are well off . . . you have no need to steal," cried Mandy, confused by all this.

"Oh, but you are wrong. What m'father gives ain't quite what I want, and what's more, I got into debt . . . more debt than you can imagine. Had to pay it off or go to debtors' prison. There was nothing for it. Now shut up, Amanda, I want that diary."

"She don't have it," said Elly. "We didn't bring it with us."

"That's right," agreed Amanda. "I buried it before we came here . . . I buried it along the way!"

"Where?" he spat at her.

"At the Abbey ruins. I'll have to show you for you'll never find it on your own."

"Very well," he said going for Elly. He shoved her onto the floor and, reaching into a cache in the wall, produced a length of rope. After tying her securely, he pushed Amanda. "Come on then . . . show me."

"What of Elly?" she stalled.

"We'll be back, Amanda—and then I shall attend to you both. Come along!" He pushed the pistol into her back roughly so that she could not doubt his meaning.

They took to horse and were at the Abbey some fifteen minutes later. Mandy did not take the horses to their hidden stables, but left them tethered to a section of crumbling wall and began contemplating the correct direction.

As the duke stood in the viscount's halls, he made a sudden decision and went flying up the stairs to his room. When next he appeared below, he had donned his long dark cape and had a pistol tucked into his cummerbund. He made purposefully for the stables where his black stallion was readied, and the livery boys watched in silent awe as he rode off.

"Prime blood, that one!" remarked one of the lads.

"Eh, that be true enough. That black'un be some piece of flesh and bone!"

"Aw, go on, sure he be, but was meaning the duke!"

"Coo . . . ye be right there!"

Mandy led her cousin round the crumbling walls to the old Abbey's center pit. Her pink slippers were nearly destroyed with mud and tearing at the seams. She pretended to slip and caught herself against a stone pillar. Her cousin came up hard behind her.

"I'm no fool, Amanda! That little bit was contrived! Now get that damned book!"

"Alfred, I was not the one who hid it . . . Elly did that part of it. I only watched. And can't you see the state of my slippers? I tripped!"

"Damn you for a cockatrice! If Elly hid it, why did you choose to come in her stead?"

"You *are* a fool! I am stalling for time, of course," she said sweetly.

He slapped her across her cheek, leaving a red mark, "Get it, chit . . . *now!*"

She had left some books behind in their secret chamber but was loath to go below with him. But she was also afraid of the look in his eyes, afraid of the meanness of his spirit. However, she needed more time. Time for the duke to return to the Manor and discover she was gone. Time for him to sense she might be here at the Abbey. He would sense it—he had to!

"Very well then." She led him to the room they had used as stables, and he followed, wide-eyed as she lifted the panel door in the floor and began the descent.

They took the stone steps down into the darkness, but he reached out and held her against him. "No tricks, Amanda!"

"I merely wanted to light a candle . . . we kept some here," she said, trying to pull away. But he kept a hold on her as she found the store of candles and matches and made a light.

He went with her into the chamber she and Ned had used, and he said, "Well, well . . . you had a cozy little home here, didn't you." His hand slipped round her waist. "You know, Amanda . . . a wife

can't testify against her husband. You could try and
convince me to let you live."

She was revolted at his touch, but time—she needed
time . . . "Now how could I manage such a feat,
Alfred?"

He smiled thickly at her as he turned her body
round and pressed her to himself. "By giving me a bit
of sugar instead of spice." He brought his mouth down
hard on hers and, even to save her life, she couldn't
take it. She beat at his chest, and managed to pull
herself away, spitting at him.

"Oh, God! I hate you! Don't you ever, ever come
near me. If you need me dead, then do it, for I'll not
try to convince you otherwise!"

"So be it, Amanda. But first, the diary . . . and
then my dear . . . " He glanced at the straw bed,
"All will come about in good time."

"Will it?" asked a deep male voice behind him.

Alfred whirled round with surprise and brought up
his gun. He fired but he was too late. The duke had
been ready for such action and had thrown up a
wooden stool, deflecting the pistol's aim. Speenham
brought his weapon round for another shot and again
was too late, for the duke fired his own, and Alfred
Speenham crumpled to the cold floor. He brought up
his head as the duke snatched away the pistol from his
hand, and he sneered.

Mandy watched horrified as her cousin's head rolled
onto his chest, and then she ran into the duke's arms
and gave vent to her emotions.

Chapter Eighteen

Mandy stood rigidly before her Uncle Bevis. Her dark eyes were filled with sympathy, as was her open heart. Yet a part of her would always remember the role he played during her brother's troubles. It had been a week since Alfred Speenham's death. The gold had been recovered, and Ned had been cleared. The gossipmongers were in their glory with all they had learned, and Squire Speenham had decided to take an extended tour of the Highlands in Scotland. He was at Sherborne Halls to make his peace with his niece and nephew.

"I . . . I can only say . . . I did what I thought was right. . . ." He seemed somehow older, thought Mandy, and . . . broken.

"I know," she answered, and though she wanted to point out his wrongs, kept silent. She turned to Ned. "Come, Neddy, wish Uncle Bevis a good journey."

Ned glanced sharply at her, for he felt that this was one relation he wanted to exclude from his memory. However, he would not make his sister unhappy. "Good-bye, Uncle, safe journey."

Squire Speenham turned and left the room, and the twins exchanged glances.

"It is over, Ned. We should try to forgive those who acted unkindly . . . or unwisely. After all, I suppose you did look guilty . . . and after your escapade in that horrid tavern with those . . . those outlaws . . ." she teased.

Elly came in then, and Mandy smiled warmly at her as the maid placed a tray of tea and biscuits on the coffee table. She watched her leave, saw the droop of her shoulders, and knew she still grieved. It drew a sad sigh from Mandy, which in turn made her brother look up.

"Mandy, been thinking, girl," said her brother. "With Aunt Agatha gone . . ."

"Thank God for that . . . Lord, I was never more pleased than when duke up and carted her off to her own lodgings. He is so wondrously strong. . . ."

"Yes, yes . . . but with her gone . . . and me off to Cambridge soon, you'll be here alone. And I told you, I won't have it!"

"That is all very well, Neddy, but there is not very much I can do about it," said Mandy, her eyes suddenly becoming misty.

The duke had said he would be leaving the viscount's manor now that Skip was off on honeymoon with his wife. She wondered idly what he would do once back in London without his wards to bother him.

"That won't do, m'girl," said Neddy frowning, "What I mean is you're near twenty-one. Will be a spinster if I leave you up in these hills. Made up m'mind to it. You've got to come down to London."

"Now, Ned, we've been through this. There is no possible way. I have no one in London to sponsor me."

"You have me!" said the duke glibly as he strode into the room.

He was looking magnificent in a short-tailed coat of powder blue, knee breeches of the same, and shining black hessians. His gleaming black hair waved about his head in perfect disorder and his black lashes shaded his blue eyes. She caught her breath, then blushed at her thoughts. She averted her eyes as she came forward to greet him. "Oh, have you come to say good-bye?" She was trying to be brave. She knew it, even Ned knew it, for she desperately wanted the duke to stay or, better yet, to show her he felt something of what she felt for him. She barely noticed that Sir Owen had entered in the duke's company, until Sir Owen somewhat quizzically called her attention.

"By Jove, Mandy, you look ravishing. Marry me and make me a happy man," he said, only edging it with a tease to bring out her smile.

"Sir Owen!" she said, surprised at the sight of him. "One does not propose to a girl with an audience about!" she returned in a bantering tone, determined to keep things between them light.

"Very well, then, come do a tour of the grounds with me," he said, but this time his voice was sincere, meaningful.

She looked at him full, meeting his hazel eyes. "I can't, Sir Owen. It is not possible . . . ever."

He was already expecting this, for he had seen the way she had been looking at the duke, and he had already some time ago noted the duke's interest in her. "Ah—I go then—with a broken heart."

She laughed. "But where . . . ?"

"To Ascot . . . to make m'fortune. I am you know, a gamester!" He donned his hat and bade them farewell before disappearing through the door.

"I like him," said Ned, "always have, you know. Jolly chap!"

"Indeed." Mandy's voice was a little sad.

The duke dismissed this with a shrug and brought the issue back to points.

"I was saying, you have me to sponsor you in London. As your guardian, that is most certainly what I intend to do."

"But . . . but you are a man," said Mandy, blushing furiously.

"And I am not without female relatives to play hostess. We leave, all three of us and Chauncy, for London on the morrow," said the duke in a tone that meant he had made up his mind.

Ned stood up, for the duke had given him a sign, and he well understood what it meant.

"Think I'll go give m'horse some exercise then."

Mandy waited for her brother to leave before saying, "You needn't go to such trouble, you know. Your guardianship ends in another month."

"I have been counting the days," he said earnestly.

She put up her chin. "I am sorry it has been such a chore!" He went to her suddenly and put his arms round her waist, then kissed her. When at length this had been accomplished he said, his voice low, husky, "You must see how impossible it is for me . . . as your guardian . . . when I would much rather be your husband!"

She cried then and pulled at his lapels. He disengaged the hold and kissed her hand.

"My darling . . . did you doubt it?"

"No . . . yes . . . when suddenly you wouldn't hold me or speak to me of anything but family affairs. I thought myself mistaken . . ."

"I was attempting to be a gentleman," he said with a laugh.

"Blister it! I don't want a gentleman . . . I want you!" They laughed over this, and he pinched her cheek.

"Gamine . . . my own gamine . . . and *I want you!*"

ℛomantic Fiction

*If you like novels of passion and daring adventure
that take you to the very heart of human drama, these
are the books for you.*

☐	AFTER—Anderson	Q2279	1.50
☐	THE DANCE OF LOVE—Dodson	23110-0	1.75
☐	A GIFT OF ONYX—Kettle	23206-9	1.50
☐	TARA'S HEALING—Giles	23012-0	1.50
☐	THE DEFIANT DESIRE—Klem	13741-4	1.75
☐	LOVE'S TRIUMPHANT HEART—Ashton	13771-6	1.75
☐	MAJORCA—Dodson	13740-6	1.75

Buy them at your local bookstores or use this handy coupon for ordering:

A-20